PUSHKIN PRESS CLASSICS

IN rARTHEST SEAS

'A book for those who know that the
best time to take a walk in a cemetery
is when you're wildly in love'
CATHERINE LACEY

'Romano writes in a dreamlike present, which is
to say the present that appears to us in dreams…
clear and full of shadows, concrete and out of reach'
NATALIA GINZBURG

'Perfection… the best introduction to the world
of a novelist who turns away from the novel and
rediscovers it in the intimate heart of her own life'
LE MONDE

'Romano's best book, a masterpiece:
writing that scorches like a blast furnace'
L'UNITÀ

LALLA ROMANO (1906–2001) was an Italian novelist, poet, translator and visual artist. Initially more active as a painter, from the 1940s Romano turned increasingly to writing, publishing her first poetry collection in 1941. During the Second World War she returned to her home province of Cuneo and became involved with the partisans. Her first novel, *Maria*, was published in 1953, and she went on to become one of Italy's most renowned writers, earning the Pavese Prize and the Strega Prize before her death at the age of 94. Her novel *A Silence Shared*, in Brian Robert Moore's translation, is also available from Pushkin Press.

BRIAN ROBERT MOORE has translated works by acclaimed Italian authors such as Michele Mari, Lalla Romano and Goliarda Sapienza. For his translations, he has received the O. Henry Prize and two PEN Translates Awards, among other honours. His translation of Lalla Romano's *A Silence Shared* was runner-up for the 2024 John Florio Prize and shortlisted for the 2023 Warwick Prize for Women in Translation.

IN FARTHEST SEAS

LALLA ROMANO

TRANSLATED FROM THE ITALIAN
BY BRIAN ROBERT MOORE

PUSHKIN PRESS CLASSICS

Pushkin Press
Somerset House, Strand
London WC2R 1LA

Original text copyright © Lalla Romano Estate
Published by arrangement with The Italian Literary Agency
English translation and end notes © 2025 Brian Robert Moore

In Farthest Seas was first published as *Nei mari estremi*
by Mondadori in Milan, 1987

First published by Pushkin Press in 2025

ISBN 13: 978-1-80533-235-0

Quest'opera è stata tradotta con il contributo del Centro per
il libro e la lettura del Ministero della Cultura italiano

All rights reserved. No part of this publication may be reproduced,
stored in a retrieval system or transmitted in any form or by any
means, electronic, mechanical, photocopying, recording or otherwise,
without prior permission in writing from Pushkin Press.

A CIP catalogue record for this title is available from the British Library

The authorised representative in the EEA is
eucomply OÜ, Pärnu mnt. 139b-14, 11317, Tallinn, Estonia,
hello@eucompliancepartner.com, +33757690241

Designed and typeset by Tetragon, London
Printed and bound in the United Kingdom by Clays Ltd, Elcograf S.p.A.

Pushkin Press is committed to a sustainable future for our
business, our readers and our planet. This book is made from
paper from forests that support responsible forestry.

www.pushkinpress.com

1 3 5 7 9 8 6 4 2

CONTENTS

PART ONE *Four Years*   7
PART TWO *Four Months*   51

Afterword 1994   181
Notes   183

PART ONE
FOUR YEARS

1

It was Silvia – she had discovered him before I did – who told me: 'Look at his hands while he talks.'

He was standing there, legs slightly apart (with hiking boots, we were in the mountains); he was telling a story, one hand held against his chest, the other raised. His hands were big and long, his fingers together, extended; and his gesturing, almost hieratic. Maybe the story was one to laugh at, a declaration along the lines of 'My sisters are two boneheads.'

For our tastes at the time – mine and Silvia's – that stylization of the gesture and hands, clearly spontaneous, was attractive, exciting. And he, immediately different from our usual companions on those hikes, who were so uninspiring.

2

The information Gigi had given my parents – they hadn't asked him for any – was the following: our new hiking companion came from Milan, he was already earning nine hundred lire a month and was the son of the Colonel of the Carabinieri.

All three pieces of information bore no interest for me. Only, I was somewhat put off by the presence of a colonel. On the Alpine Club excursions there were girls who always wanted to walk in front of everyone because 'the daughters of colonels have to be first'.

In terms of Milan, it must have been important then, too, because it set the fashion trends. He wore a hat with a bright-coloured ribbon (everyone else's was black) and the street kids would jeer at him. To tell the truth, on this point I sided with Cuneo's street kids, who were provincial and conservative.

I had even been bothered by his white cloth cap, round with a turned-up brim like in the American Navy, when I saw him for the first time on the tram for Demonte. On top of that, he was playing a kind of harmonica. How young he was! I felt old and rotten.

3

The first signs that he had of our existence had been rather comical. Gigi, who had a sense of humour but was still one of Cuneo's right-minded citizens, had started warning him: 'The Romano girls will be there. We'll have to behave.'

And another little incident had given him a curious idea about our family. The usual friends – I wasn't there – were going up the Stura Valley, and just outside Demonte he noticed with surprise a little hill left partially wild and partially cultivated, encircled by an imposing wall formed by lots of concrete balusters, and on the hilltop a kind of terrace resting on four pillars adorned with creepers. 'Why, who could all that belong to?' he asked. 'It's ours,' Silvia said, and he thought that she was trying to be funny. But Gigi confirmed it. In fact, the strange hill was 'the Estate' for us, and that little terrace was 'the Pinnacle'. Up there, my father had dreamed of building a villa.

4

He had discovered them, before really discovering me. After a hike, we were returning on the tram from Demonte, and they had come down from Boves to wait for us at the Borgo station. He, through the tram window, saw them and was struck. 'Who in the world are those two people?' 'They're the Romano girls' parents.'

He was shocked, he told me later, actually indignant that such extraordinary people could be named so nonchalantly, almost with disregard.

They were standing there, still, and smiling in silence. Her eyes, bright and deep, made her beauty mysterious; and Papà, who was older, with his handlebar moustache, certainly had a festive and indulgent air about him. They were smiling as though out of a sort of altruistic happiness, naive and at the same time noble. They seemed great people to him, like royals, and yet simple, kind.

Their unchanged presence – sudden and dizzying – appeared to him a long time after. They had been dead for years. It was once again an apparition: a dream. He told it to me right away – at night – still in the grip of fear and joy: 'The doorbell rings, and I go to answer. It's them, smiling as always, but soaking from the rain. "Come in," I say, "come in and dry yourselves." They say, "No, we have to go. We just want to tell you that everything is okay now. We're together." I can't remember the exact words now, but that's more or less what they said. And I felt a great sense of peace, of security. Even if it was very sad that they didn't want to come in, and I understood that I wouldn't see them again.'

5

On the hikes, I was the favourite of the leader, the small (in stature), energetic and amusing Gigi. And so I was invited – I alone – to climb the famous Meja with the boys.

There's a little photograph. I'm crouched down between the two jagged edges of a couloir, my braids hanging down over my white shirt. While I was there, he (we called him Monti) handed me two tiny edelweiss flowers: 'These are for the signorina.'

Years later he told me that I had looked like Minnehaha. I was still flattered by this. Minnehaha was the daughter of an Indian chief, and it hadn't been all that many years since we'd grown out of Salgari's books.

6

Our first conversation was in Boves, on what was referred to as the road of the Madonna, because it led to the church Madonna dei Boschi. Silvia walked in front of us with Detto, who was courting her a bit; he had come to accompany Detto, his friend at the time. They had gone to Venice together for the Biennale, and they showed us photos in which a girl appeared. I was always annoyed when other girls were referenced in my presence, and this time, too, their trip immediately lost all interest for me.

So, walking after dinner on that road, he spoke of Modigliani. Everyone talked about him in those days, and everyone (the foolish ones, which is to say almost everyone) acted outraged: the long necks, the flat colours, et cetera. I loved Modigliani deeply then; but he couldn't have known this, he didn't know anything about me. I mean that the topic wasn't aimed at pleasing me. He spoke of Modigliani with admiration, in a grave, serious tone: and he didn't know that 'admiring Modigliani' (what that meant) was truly what mattered in life, for me.

Maybe this first real exchange was somewhat similar to that other fateful one with Giovanni. But Modigliani was much more important to me than Kant had been then.

The road – the woods on one side, on the other the meadows – would have been dark, had it not been for the moon. On the way back (the two of us ahead) we had before us, unfurled in the sky, the plough of the Great Bear. For my whole life since then, it has helped me gauge my personal situation in the cosmos.

7

I was unfearing, on the bicycle. That bicycle was our habitual means of transportation. Once again the road was named for 'the Madonna of the woods', after the Madonna dei Boschi.

> There sleeps, encircled by dreaming woods,
> a far-off city

began an unwritten poem.

I was near another village that was still under the shadow of the Bisalta, Cuneo's mountain; it wasn't really a road so much as a stony mule track. On my way back, the descent kept growing steeper and steeper, and I kept rolling faster down: the brakes had stopped working. At a sharp turn I became frightened, and I suddenly decided to throw myself to the ground. I don't know if he was the one to lift me up; I know that he was standing there, and I, panting, leaned against his chest – sturdy but not stiff, warm and at the same time fresh. I could feel his heart beating.

The next month in Paris I had a big round bruise on my arm. My dark red dress was made of silk voile, very low cut, with drooping points at the bottom and shoulders. The dress matched the colour of my bruise. I was at the Café de Paris with Lionello Venturi; the tall and gallant violinist came over to ask me what I wanted to hear, and I suggested Veracini's *Largo* (a musical choice that had to do with Boves).

8

Back from Paris, I had – seemingly out of necessity – an excuse to see him. That he worked in a bank was supremely indifferent to me; if anything, slightly comical.

I laid on the counter – it was the first time I'd set foot in a bank – my French bills, and the coins too. My nonchalance was ignorance; a grouch of a man – whom I judged 'the manager' – grew irritated and pushed back the coins: you couldn't exchange those. I nonetheless had the gall to ask for him. Now I know that my assuredness was not so much for the importance I gave to my *retour de Paris*, as for the electrifying expectation of astonishing him, of witnessing his emotion. He appeared, pale, and astonished, yes, but, it seemed to me, painfully so. What I noticed right away, and it made him seem infinitely pitiable to me, was, on the lapel of his jacket – not one of his usual ones, but grey, a bit shabby – a few pointed pins. Almost as though his job were humble, servile, like a shop boy, a tailor's apprentice. But once I was outside, my cruel jubilance immediately stamped out that pity. I murmured to myself, as I crossed the piazza, the words of a little song, heard who knows when: 'You're pale, you're pale, you're pale for me…'

9

I was crossing the piazza, alone, and I saw him from afar, with someone. When I was a few paces from him he broke away and came towards me. He said that they would be going – he and Gigi – to the Pagarì, if I wanted to join them. It was even better than a declaration of love: I was considered *equal*, and surely they hadn't forgotten that I was a woman. It had already happened for the Meja; but this time, whose idea had it been?

The Pagarì Refuge, legendary to us all, was a tiny cabin at a three-thousand-metre altitude, held there with steel cables. ('You mountaineers in the Maritime Alps put your cabins up on the peaks,' the great Mezzalama once said.)

It was November, we needed to light the wood stove. He chopped wood in a little clearing and grew warm from this exertion, so that, despite the cold, his shirt gleamed white in the twilight. There was something at once adventurous, exotic (in the sense of far-away countries) and intimate in that image, as though already lived (or dreamed). It matched, or rather expressed all the risk and mystery there was in that cold light, in that solitude. In the stories by Lawrence that I had just read, I had found this; and for a moment I felt an attraction for him that was violent, secret, but I believe already tenaciously deep. It wasn't an idea, it was a sensation: head-spinning, but not unsettling. Rather, familiar.

That night, each bundled up in thorny military blankets like three giant newborns or dead sailors about to be lowered into the sea, we lay in a row – I in the middle – on the higher floor, I suppose to receive a little residual warmth. From a small window some feeble light entered. In the wild wind the walls, the steel cables, everything vibrated, whistled, hissed. Motionless on their backs, my two companions had their wool brims lowered all the way down to their noses and were sleeping: or were pretending to. In the glimmering trail of light I could make out his profile, which looked funny to me. I laughed silently to myself. I was – who knows why – happy.

10

The next day we climbed – with our skis – the glacier under the Maledia, all the way to the Pagarì Pass. Up there, crouched close together for warmth, we stayed awhile: to contemplate, in the sky, a city. A city of clouds. It must have changed, as clouds do, but so imperceptibly, it seemed still, immutable. Far away, but not too far. Distinctly visible were domes, obelisks, minarets: an eastern city. Its colours were delicate, soft: orange-pink, violet.

There's a tiny photograph (they were all that way back then), a piece of paper that's best examined with a magnifying glass because the image is a bit blurry. Gigi took it, obviously, on the way back. There's a narrow bridge, over a stream, made of two logs covered with brushwood and twigs, like in a valley under the Himalayas; and on that bridge, two small figures facing each other, almost as though they had crossed paths there. But they are absorbed, solitary, and just barely in relief against the reflected light. The girl, with her bag, a long skirt, skis planted next to her, looks to the side; he, skis on his shoulder, his round head in profile, pensive.

11

People used to say 'the 8th and 9th' and it meant two consecutive public holidays in December. The 8th and 9th of that year is one of the extremely rare dates in my interior history, almost completely devoid of chronological artefacts.

There was the usual mountain (near the border, at the end of my valley), the usual uninteresting, relaxing friends. The first evening, having stopped skiing because of the dark, the two of us – out of a kind of audacity – chose not to cage ourselves with the others in a car but to walk the road from Argentera to Bersezio. The road was icy, we were light, skis on our shoulders. Flurries of thick fog appeared and dissipated. There, our first kiss happened: suddenly. It was sweet, not fervent; a bit solemn, maybe, and not entirely without our knowing it. We've just broken apart when we see, coming out of that strange fog, a figure. Perhaps a magical apparition, certainly not a mystical one. A priest, with a black cassock, completely real. He greeted us, and vanished into the fog. The rather comical occurrence lightened the gravity of the moment.

Later, I was seated by the corner of the long table at the Caccia Reale, with him next to me, at the head, so that we were almost facing each other, and isolated (the others, loud, did not exist). I looked at him and met, very close to me, his golden-brown eyes. And in them a deep and warm, mysterious tenderness. A severe tenderness.

12

The next time is again in a closed space: in the room I shared with Silvia on Via Barbaroux, with the light-coloured walnut furniture that Papà had had made for us in Demonte. There was a desk in front of the window, where I sat to give Latin lessons and listen, in the unending afternoons, to the somnolent hammering of a pianola, which repeated old melancholy arias in the street. Now he is there, no doubt summoned to pose for a portrait. We embrace each other. No one will bother us, because my mother respects me, and Silvia even more so. But I am troubled; I say: 'We should leave each other. I don't want this story to end like the others.' I had disappointed Giovanni, had been disappointed by Anthony, without counting the other, let's say minor ones. Giovanni had disappeared; Anthony, at my declaration 'I have a boyfriend' (I'd seen him in Turin), had said, irritated, 'You knew that I wanted to marry you.' Irritated, not heartbroken; in any case, I hadn't believed it. Now I didn't want to disappoint him. And he – calm, almost as though he'd been expecting this – replied: 'We don't have to leave each other. We could get married.' I rested against him, but I didn't respond. He added: 'I'm not at all rich; but I'll work.' The conversation was taking a turn that I didn't like. The elegance of not using the word 'poor' wasn't lost on me, but 'rich' too, despite being accompanied by a negation, was still an economic term; and I abhorred all that was practical, and even goodwill. However, again I saw the image of him chopping wood at the Pagarì, and I found anew that guarantee of a wild life, a free and far-off life. The unlikely prospect reassured me.

13

'I'm going to San Maurizio with Monti.' 'Just the two of you?' 'Yes.' My mother looked puzzled. I said: 'We might get married.' She wasn't surprised, only replied: 'He's handsome.' As if it were a valid argument. She was austere, but fanciful; and so she was free, unpredictable.

For Mamma, San Maurizio was a name from her childhood. A flat, solitary high ground, two old churches at the top. I don't know why we had chosen it. I had never been, but I liked the name, for how she said it.

The day was grey, and it was windy and raining up there; on the way back, we came running down off the paths. I was wearing an elegant dress – for him, I imagine. I had bought it in Turin (a 'steal' suggested by Aunt Carola). It was long and smooth, black, made of very heavy and soft silk; it resembled women's dresses in fourteenth-century frescoes. It was worn with a paper-thin, turquoise-coloured scarf knotted around the neck. While I ran, the scarf slipped off, and the wind carried it away. We looked for it among the bushes and the rocks, uselessly. Since clothes managed to interest me almost exclusively as emblems, I was saddened by the loss of that veil.

In town, while we were crossing a piazza (a secondary one) – holding hands! – I realized that an 'honest' family unit, passing by at a comfortable distance, was shooting sideways glances, suspicious and icy. For all I cared…

14

Mamma said that people had commented, hinted at the situation to Papà, and that he was vexed. I knew that he was strict about these things – and not because of other people – having been a bit of a libertine in his youth. Silvia became indignant, as she always did when allegations were made against me: 'It's not like Lalla is Giovanna Celloni!'

This Giovanna was a classmate of hers who was said to corrupt the male boarders at the school opposite her home, showing herself nude at the window ('moeurs de province').

Mamma had mentioned our plan to get married, and Papà said: 'No man at twenty can know what woman is right for him.' The assertion was taken seriously by my suitor: he asked for a meeting.

They said very little to one another; the conversation was not all that different from that old one between my father and my grandfather Michele, who wasn't even able to establish the dowry, because Papà didn't want to hear anything of it.

I didn't ask what they had said, then. I found out only at the end of our life (of his and now of mine before too long).

15

He told me about a little charming and funny adventure from his first days in Cuneo. It was the summer when he had arrived after completing his high school graduation exams, with the disappointment – the despair – of not being able to continue his studies, and the impending prison of a job he hadn't chosen, devoid of interest, devoid of prospects. But he told me only that he'd go riding towards the mountains on his bicycle, to dull his senses.

At a fork in a valley, he had read the name Entracque, and mentally pronounced it as 'Antrac', because he thought it was French. He asked an old man who was hoeing in a field: 'Is this the road to Antrac?'

The old man looked at him, shrugged his shoulders and didn't reply, went back to hoeing.

I recognized the dignity of that peasant farmer who'd thought he was being mocked; but I don't know if I understood then what the little story signified, confirmed for him – that is exile, exclusion.

16

On Saturdays his mother used to lay out a white silk shirt on his bed; it meant that the next day there would be a reception at the prefect's house. The prefect had a daughter. He had gone once or twice; there was this daughter with her friends, and they played parlour games like 'what does he do – what does she do'.

Once he had started working, he said to his mother, seeing the shirt laid out on his bed: 'Now I'm a bank clerk, I'm no longer "the Colonel's son".' And the next day he went off to the mountains. I hadn't the slightest suspicion of this family drama. And in any case, it was what I called to myself the 'all too human'.

I had seen them, his parents, crossing the piazza. His father, very tall and awfully handsome, with a straight and thin nose, a lofty, bored demeanour; his wife, small, stiffly upright; in front of them walked his two baby sisters (adolescents), looking the same, with the same little red jackets. A family with a touch of a Leo Longanesi caricature to it. I only thought that it couldn't have anything to do with the wild life.

17

Detto had been educated by a tutor uncle who was a music lover, and he had studied violin. In any case, he was passionate about it. The year that Silvia and I had a room in Turin, he and Detto would come for the Regio: *The Mastersingers*, *Boris*. Detto was enthusiastic, but I liked the way Cenzo had of listening, his air of concentration, without commentary. He confided to me that he loved – like me – the diffuse sound of the orchestra trying out their instruments. For him it was a rousing preparation; whereas I liked it truly as music. I said to him that I loved piano scales, and he admitted that he hated them: he'd hear them at home, his sisters' unending exercises.

Afterwards, on and on we repeated themes and motifs, softly singing along; Detto on the violin too, I on the piano. We loved those operas with an exclusive love, as if they had been written for us or, at the very least, planned for us that season.

Innocenzo had frequented opera houses as a boy. His father had a theatre seat at his disposal, and he'd send him chaperoned by a carabiniere. He'd sit sunk in the chair, motionless and his eyes fixed forward, with the horror of being noticed, but also with rapture for the spectacle. His first opera was *Tosca*. He was ten years old and the impression it gave him was terrifying. That man in uniform was really being stabbed, was really dying, and the woman really threw herself into the void.

Many years later we listened to a *Tristan* from the Berlin Opera. The next day he said to me: 'This morning I was walking under the portico of La Scala; I stopped for a second and said to myself: inside there, last night, something great took place, something immense.'

18

That year in Turin was when the train stations assumed importance, especially the one in Cuneo; he'd accompany me to the train. It must truly have been the case that we didn't notice other people around: a friend, a hiking companion, apparently waved at us, became offended; already he felt neglected because he hadn't been told anything in confidence. Reaching me, these tragicomic pieces of news were, like all provincial murmurings, not even annoying: non-existent.

When he came to Turin on Sundays, he'd then have to leave again on what was almost a night train to get to the bank on time. I knew that he didn't go to a hotel, but waited in the station. 'How did you do it?' I asked years later; at the time I didn't know the trick (nor did I worry about it). 'I'd wind up my alarm clock' (it must have been very small, if it wasn't cumbersome during the day, but I pictured it as enormous, for a kitchen) 'then with my arms folded and my hat over my eyes, I'd sleep.'

On one of those Sundays we went up to Superga; I wanted to redo with him my outing with Andrée, which felt incredibly far away. There was still the old osteria with the floor of rough planks and the old coin-operated player piano.

19

It was a bit like we were the first human couple – or the last – for all the astonishment we provoked. Perhaps mockery too; or even hate. There were anonymous letters (like in French novels and films), immediately forgotten by us – by me – in any event.

Mr Varisella, an old man compared to us, was a kind of pleasure-loving, discreet suitor of Aunt Rina. We were standing in each other's arms in the wood, he saw us from the ski trail and remarked: 'People say that love blinds. They didn't see the snow any more and they took off their skis.'

Some were less indulgent. It was at the Passo del Van, with companions. After arriving at the top, beyond the frayed edge of the snowfield we find a stretch of dry ground in the sun. The two of us sit off on our own. In front of us there appears the famous (in Cuneo) lawyer A., who says something about our sitting off on our own, et cetera. We don't respond; in part because of something we saw which doubly isolated us.

A little earlier on the snowfield – we were at a distance from the group during the ascent, too – we made out before us, in the uniform white (in the shadows), a strand of black marks spaced apart, coming into focus as small pointed bodies: birds, swallows. Stuck in the snow. Seven of them. No doubt blinded, tricked by the white, they had missed the mark in their low flight. Or some impact, a sudden violence of the wind. The small tragic image was one of defeat, but also a transfiguration.

20

Comically heroic adventures – faced in the name of love – always amused me later, maybe even years later, when he'd happen to recall them, with his precise and at the same time fantastical way of narrating (similar to Papà's with me as a little girl).

In Boves, he'd arrive on summer evenings after going down the long tree-lined avenue on his bicycle, crossing the river on the shaking footbridge, riding back up the riverbank on the rocky road to Mellana. Once he ended up puncturing his tyre and he fixed it right there in the dark. The comical part was this: he arrived out of breath, after dinner – the bank already plagued him with overtime – and my mother made him an after-dinner coffee. But he hadn't eaten. He sipped his little mug in one go, standing up, as though it were castor oil, while I was anxious to leave.

At home he was admired most of all for his manners. 'He was so polite,' Mamma said when she was dying, and I felt remorse because he had sometimes noted certain harsh manners of mine. My baby sister Luciana (in elementary school at the time), hearing his praises sung in the family, came out with the declaration: 'He's like Cavour: "practical, prudent, resolved".'

He liked Luciana very much; he said that, had he been younger, he would have fallen in love with her; as he would have with our mother, for that matter, had he been older. He didn't say so for Silvia, who was beautiful, even: maybe not so whimsical. He then loved her a great deal in life, with a fraternal love.

21

The official proposal (the Colonel and his wife over on Via Barbaroux) changed nothing, naturally. I'd always detested, no less than now, the words: wife, husband, mother-in-law, daughter-in-law, and the like. That line in the Gospel always enchanted me: 'They will no longer be husbands and wives.' It was the same thing with the word 'engaged'; the poor use it, perhaps? But my father, of all people, used it; and not because of 'what people will say'. Enzo Paci, still in high school, would often come to see me. They had met each other, he and Cenzo, but they weren't friends. Enzo Paci had immediately sought him out, as soon as he showed up in Cuneo, because he'd heard about his impressive eight in philosophy during his graduation exams. But Innocenzo had brushed it aside.

Now I think that the way he refrained from 'talking philosophy' must already have been rooted in his avoiding vanity, including in what seems to be, on the contrary, the most serious of topics. He revealed this, dying, with one of the last things he said, a sentence seemingly elusive and instead deeply affirmative of his rigour, of his wry wisdom and humility.

I had always declared that I wanted a man who was philosophical, but clean, elegant in fact. Was it therefore more important, someone who admired Modigliani? Could be – there was passion in me, for painting. Either way, I liked him and that was that.

Papà pointed out to me, in a serious if not stern manner, that now that I was engaged it wasn't suitable for me to have a boy over. I certainly must have responded testily; my assuredness – setting aside my *sacred* freedom – was founded on something real: I didn't like Enzo Paci.

Later in life, on the subject of interesting men, Cenzo said once: 'At a certain point, you no longer see their faces.' Cutting. However, it was not Enzo's face, which happened to be beautiful, intense, but something else: his skin? The undefinable but heavy message of his body never attracted me. I was flattered by his indirect confession (of love), passed on to me by an entrusted friend, but it cost me nothing to disappoint him.

22

And so they had come; my mother immediately liked his father the Colonel. I know – she was like me in these things – that she liked him because he was handsome, and very, very gentlemanly. The Colonel was dispassionate, ironic, pessimistic. Papà was witty, teasing: he was certainly going to get bored chatting with the Colonel. In any case, Mamma, after making a reference in her rapid, allusive and enchanted way to the Colonel's allure, repeated to me a remark he'd made. A confidential, familiar remark, which was already strange, but even more so because of how uncouth it was. 'I'll have to walk hunched for years.' I don't really know whether there was only understanding in my mother's voice, or a shade of resentment too: the engagement seen as a family disgrace. Then, I felt only a certain degree of surprise over that kind of behaviour, and even a bit of fondness for the austere Colonel for having dropped his guard. Right after came irritation, and I let it go: I didn't worry about making sense of it. I didn't even realize that, behind that grievance, there was a will which was in a certain sense merciless: that of Innocenzo. Who knows how many years it took me to grasp something, after patient – on his part – hints at the facts. True, at the time he had kept silent about it with me; he knew that I wouldn't have borne it, that I wouldn't have wanted to marry him any more. I began to understand, or at least to consider the problem somewhat clearly when I heard this final judgement come from him: 'People in the military understand nothing of civilian life.' Thus he absolved them – I thought – of having sacrificed him for his siblings. Except that 'absolve' is a concept of mine; he cast no blame on them.

23

It must have been directly after the engagement became official that I was invited to take a trip in a car with him and his father; the Colonel needed to inspect a border post. We were in an open-top car, the two of us behind in the wind.

In the few moments that I was granted to observe the Colonel in his presumably bureaucratic duties, I glimpsed the enchantment of authority. Not real – furthermore, military – authority, but rather a kind of regality, as with certain great actors 'of silence', who on stage impersonate kings (mostly Shakespearean ones).

Aunt Rina, the caustic woman, found he had an 'ecclesiastic' air about him, like a bishop. Being very Catholic herself, the observation couldn't have been intended to mock him; and yet I felt it as somehow withering: but, again, she was caustic.

24

We had planned a hike in the famous Valley of Marvels. We didn't make it to these marvels; and it was strange, we had never given up before, never failed to reach our goal. It was because I felt, little by little, an insurmountable weariness come over me. It had something mysterious to it. Only after our wedding night, that is, after the 'real' labours of love, did I think back on my exhaustion that day. But there was another coincidence. Walking on that trail – which wasn't steep, but sunken in the rock – he had lifted me up, and had carried me a little in his arms. And this act of lifting me – I was thin and didn't weigh much – was in fact something he repeated many times, later, during my moments of amorous weariness.

All this is also a preamble to what now – in these days in which I've recalled our unconcluded journey in the Valley of Marvels – happened to me in a dream. I've been walking through a high city, flanked by mountains, I believe my mountains. I've recognized Ronvello, the path, Monfieis. I realize that I've strayed too far; to get back to the city, I have to return on a long, sunny road. In the evening I find myself in the city, which I think must be Parma, one of 'his' cities. I ask for the main street, I recognize the buildings (never seen before). A man shows me a guesthouse, and he continues to accompany me when I leave; then in a piazza I say goodbye to him. The piazza stretches uphill, high up on the left I see Innocenzo, I'd like to say so to my guide; instead I run towards

Innocenzo, we hug each other; I say: 'I've been walking since this morning, I haven't eaten, but I'm not tired.' He lifts me up in his arms.

25

I was with Silvia on Corso Nizza, so empty and sun-drenched in those days. She looked at me and said, with an expression of shock and admiration: 'You seem like Tess!'

It was a grave thing to say. We had just read *Tess of the d'Urbervilles*: what she meant I don't know, but it helped me define my somewhat dreamy state, between blissful and distressed. Almost as though I were truly going to be 'sacrificed', even if 'crowned with flowers'. I had never said it to myself, but I thought, or rather I felt, that getting married was something fatal, abyssal in fact, a kind of death. I intuited a sense of risk, which was exhilarating too, but detached from me, from our story. Almost an investiture: for some unknown end.

26

So that it would be the least public possible, we decided to have the ceremony in Boves, where we spent our summers, in August, his month off work. The church was the Madonna dei Boschi, our first walk. Coming out of the church, there were three panting girls with a bicycle; Luciana told me afterwards that they were the girls from the 'little cannon' (so we called the Golden Cannon Hotel, which was opposite us on Via Barbaroux in Cuneo); they were disappointed to have arrived late.

I had a silk dress, lilac-coloured – my colour – and an exotic straw hat (a straw called Bangkok), which had a ruffled lilac veil made of silk between the bowl and the brim. Only Uncle Alessio, who was always intemperate, cheered, 'To the newlyweds!' No photographs were taken, and so it was never settled whether I wore my braids down over my chest, as I always did, or my hair up. The disagreement was between my aunts and Innocenzo; I don't remember how the opinions were split, but I know that he'd end the discussion with the laughably chivalrous line: 'I would know – I'm the one who married her!'

A few years later, while I was painting by the road for Sant'Antonio in Boves, next to a row of vineyards, some people passed behind my easel, and I caught a young woman saying loudly: 'She got married at the Madonna, a very romantic wedding.' Surely she was a romantic girl; and the man walking with her – her husband? – was someone who, one night, passing beneath my balcony while I undressed, had sung:

> When in the night sky
> the stars do glow
> and off to bed
> the pretty girls go.

27

From that day the thought that followed me and also persecuted me a bit over the years was for my mother. Everyone: his family, that is the Colonel, his wife, the two silly girls crying like fountains, the two serious-looking young boys; mine: Papà, Mamma, Silvia and Luciana, my grandparents, my aunts, Uncle Alessio, my uncle the doctor and his wife – everyone at the wedding reception having lunch on the terrace under the Concord grape pergola. I always wondered who had helped Mamma: Cia was married and had small children. I asked eventually, and every time they replied: 'You know that she always pulled off miracles.'

In that thought of my own neglect converged the innumerable other instances (from all the other days) when she did everything without drawing any attention to herself, and festively.

That day I was only anxious to get away. The party was for me, and sentimental. How horrifying. Detto accompanied us to the train station in Cuneo. I knew that Innocenzo had planned the trip with him, keeping in mind our tastes and the costs, which had to be modest. I didn't have any idea where we'd go, and I didn't care. Maybe they told me the names of the places. I knew only that the first station was called Desenzano. The name sounded musical.

28

That evening, in Desenzano, we were walking by the lake in a moonlit fog. That thing had to take place. He had always abstained – there's no doubt – only out of respect; and he regretted it many times, sounding a mix of melancholic and humorous. We had secretly been to Rome for three days! If I had neither proposed nor anticipated it, that was because the thing didn't appeal to me, didn't even intrigue me. That moment, kept secret and therefore mysterious, perturbed me; above of all because of my fear of not being good enough. And all the more that evening in Desenzano. There was the vague fear of the biological event and the embarrassment of coming across as too ignorant, obtuse, rather unfeeling. Whether he might have problems of his own wasn't something I asked myself. It was true that on another, much more magical night, not with a lake moon (ambiguous and veiled) but a harsh, limpid, blinding moon on an icy road, back when Detto was courting reluctant Silvia, and they were walking ahead, far ahead (they weren't stopping to kiss each other), he'd confessed to me – what? That he'd never possessed a woman. Certainly that wasn't how he said it; what did he say? I didn't want to hear. I knew that he had never wanted the girls in brothels; and so, who?

I didn't think of this, on that slightly dreamy walk in Desenzano; but I would have done without the thing. We didn't speak of it.

29

What it left was an impression of discomfort, effort, labour. Something technical like an operation (a surgical one), in the overly harsh light: in fact, it's necessary in operations. Afterwards, I fell asleep with my head on his shoulder, as I always would from then on, in the hollow between his shoulder and his chest. I had a fleeting thought, sparked by a physical sensation: his silk shirt smelled slightly acidic. (His smell was fragrant like the aroma of fresh bread.) His mother, I thought, gave him a shirt made of artificial silk.

As that boy of Bresson's said right before having himself killed at Père Lachaise: 'I thought at a time like this I'd have sublime thoughts; instead, do you know what I'm thinking about?' (but his friend shoots). My story doesn't contain 'the devil, probably'; nor is a wedding night as grave as an execution.

30

It just happened; I don't know what to say. Nor do I know *how* it came to pass that in the rustic room with a creaking floor (I've forgotten the town's name) I felt such bliss. Already in Riva, the night after Desenzano, it had been beautiful; even a little exalting. He had lifted me up under my armpits and placed me standing on top of a truncated column by the side of the stairs: to make a monument of me? And there were those songs which were so sad in the restaurant garden.

In that sun-filled room in the town with no name, I no longer felt coarse or embarrassed. And I was even proud of the perfume I'd bought in Cuneo at the famous shop owned by the Meinero brothers, who entertained their clients by flirting with them (even austere Aunt Rina, for example, would go on discussing gloves for ages). I had asked for something that wasn't sweet-smelling. It was a tiny bottle – it must have been expensive – and its light and bitter aroma (might it have been for a man?) mixed with the scent of pine in the room. I was also happy about the name of the hotel: Seven Parish Churches. For me it came from the world of the Brothers Grimm. Then for the rest of our life we recalled the owner, a young woman who never smiled, but who always asked: 'Did you have enough to eat?'

The church in the woods was called Madonna di Lares. It was a larch wood, and therefore bright and not 'Brothers Grimm'; the ground beneath was covered in red cyclamen, with that smell of theirs (in my mountains there were none). As with the Marvels, we never made it to Malga Cengledin: and this time, too, for a strange weariness in me. The Malga was high up, I felt I was suffocating amid the tall grass, my heart racing like mad. It never happened again, after that.

31

In Venice, where everything is painting, I was swept back up in my primary passion. We were going up the Canal Grande in a steamboat – it was night – and a vision became etched in my memory, one that also corresponded to legend. In front of a sumptuous palazzo (which?) on the pier or whatever it's called, jutting out over the water, a woman with flowing red hair lay stretched on a sofa, violently illuminated. She was playing solitaire, and she seemed a witch to me.

I wandered around on my own all day, because he was unwell. I suggested he have broth, I thought the sick were supposed to be given broth. They had no broth in the hotel. Under the windows flowed a stinking canal. It was truly a bit 'death in Venice'.

From the many trips there that followed, I want to recall an image. An image that could appear anywhere but which we contemplated at length, in silence, with a special happiness after something painful that I can't remember, from a window in the Grünwald Hotel. A big, immense cloud, orangish pink.

Like other visions that you don't forget, this one, too, had a double. Another big cloud, majestic and pinkish, which I contemplated for a long while with a mysterious, seemingly unjustified happiness, with baby Emiliano (from here, above the ugly buildings opposite).

32

After Venice, in Tortona at his grandfather's. I knew he liked this grandfather of his. Maybe at the time I still didn't know the story of the letter.

His parents had already gone to Cuneo and he had stayed in Milan to take his graduation exams (at the age of seventeen, like me, for that matter). In a little room he would cook himself one egg for lunch and another for dinner. During his examinations multiple professors had invited him to their universities. But his father had given him a letter for a man in Piazza della Scala. The incredible thing for me is this: the envelope was open and he didn't read the letter. 'Do you want to work in a bank?' the man in Piazza della Scala asked him. His blood froze. He immediately thought of his grandfather, took the train to Tortona; but his grandfather argued back: 'Your father must have his reasons.'

And yet his grandfather loved him, because he was his only studious grandchild. When he stayed with him in Milan, Innocenzo would show him around the city, and then he'd have to study at night. In any case, he was incapable of holding a grudge, and his grandfather was hard not to like.

When he was a little boy, he'd go see his grandfather while he was in the courts in Voghera. There was a famous fancy pastry shop (if you frequented it, you were socially all right); cavalry officers would loiter out front, their gloved hands resting on the hilts of their sabres; and his grandfather: 'Look at those spongers!'

His son Edoardo, Innocenzo's father, wanted to go to the Military Academy; he was displeased by the idea, but he was liberal and didn't stop him. His son's story, too, was a sorry one: after a few months at the Academy, he discovered that he didn't love that environment at all, but he kept quiet and so it was for his whole life. During the Great War, my mother-in-law would weep because she never received any news from the front; and Innocenzo's grandfather would say: 'He wanted to go into the military: war is his trade!'

33

His grandfather was a thin man, quick-witted, very distinguished; a bitter, aristocratic face. He lived alone. His home, which I never saw, was the ugliest place in the world for Innocenzo (like Tortona, for that matter). He ate at a trattoria, and invited us there. The simpleton of a waiter seemed scared to death: 'Is your grandfather mean?' I asked. 'No, but he enjoys nagging people.' Innocenzo hated Tortona because during his years in Perugia his father would bring the whole family there for vacation, to be close to his grandfather. Leaving those beautiful places for that ugly town: this had been hard for him to accept.

But the most extraordinary story about his grandfather was this. He'd had an incredibly sweet wife; he, however, frequented the cafés, the social clubs, with her always at home. When she died, he mourned her with a passionate, mysterious devotion. Every day he spent hours – hours! – at the cemetery, sitting on a chair in the room-shaped tomb.

When Innocenzo was in Tortona, he'd go with him and stay standing behind his chair. For me it was a joy that he too – like me in Demonte – had grown intimately familiar with the cemetery.

34

'When we entered our home, Maria was already there. We had come back from our honeymoon, and we walked on tiptoes, because it was midnight.'

(from *Maria*)

PART TWO
FOUR MONTHS

1

By a rough hand we are pushed
reluctant animals
chased from the warmth of a den
onto windswept roads
(…)

2

I cannot receive his images of beauty, from our happy life together: I have to cross those of sickness and death. I have to start from all the times I thought he might die.

The first time – not in Venice, where he seemed to have come down with something the way one does as a child, which doesn't mean anything, and in fact I'd suggested broth (as a cure) in that nightmare hotel on the canal – the first time was in our home on the avenue, when he came in looking pale, later than usual (maybe they brought him home). That was it: pale.

My uncle the doctor came, who was small in stature and annoyed about the fact: he said that his heart was fatigued because in people who are too tall it needs to pump more. (My uncle restored his honour the first night our child was sick, when I was frantic because I didn't know what to give him, and he suggested dipping a little piece of gauze in sugared water for him to suck on.)

As for Innocenzo's heart, it was so strong that, in the agony of death, it could not cease to beat. His agony. Even the last, the supreme (mortal) malady revealed itself through pallor.

3

In one of those long, silent nights in our home on the avenue, I was woken by shouts: 'Burglars!' 'Wake up,' I shake him, 'there are burglars!' 'Where?' 'Downstairs, at the seamstresses'.' (There were seamstresses there too, like on Via Barbaroux and at my great-uncle the priest's home; behind, in a small, low house.) He gets up, goes to the window, leans out of it; the shouts dissipate, die out; he waits a little, and falls back asleep, resting on the windowsill.

And the same thing the night I gave birth: he wouldn't wake up. I called him, touched him, I was almost afraid (for myself). When he understood, he ran – no, he didn't actually run – to call for my mother all the way on Via Barbaroux and the midwife, I think (who scared me).

He was so young! When he went to the municipality offices to declare the birth, the civil servant squared him up and down, said: 'Send me the father.' Youth is not always beautiful; but he was: and he seemed untouchable.

Precisely in that large, bright and tranquil bedroom, I had a premonition. At night, naturally. And it must have been a dream. I saw Death at the foot of the bed, on my side: a nun. It was Mère Consolata, smiling. In Turin, at the Faithful Companions, we girls considered her false; her unwavering smile, stamped and pulled across her face, seemed phony to us.

I didn't remember, then, Casetta's dream; only now does it come back to me. Casetta was droll, extremely intelligent. And she was devoted to me. We were classmates in school, and then at university. After that she disappeared, I don't know how or where. She had told me in a long letter that she'd dreamt my wedding. The groom was brown-haired, and I was happy. But the coach was one for mourning and the horses were draped in black.

4

When we had recently been married, he translated Joyce's 'The Dead' for me. Does snow fall, in that story? (Or maybe we read it while it snowed.) I've always connected the two.

And also once with the *Hammerklavier*; I said to my close friend Turin, who was dying, how beautiful it was to listen to that sonata while it snows outside, and I thought: while someone is dying. In *A Silence Shared*, too, there is snow as death, and death as peace.

5

It was not in illnesses that I feared losing him; but in absences, in distance. To die is to move off into the distance: I'd find this out later.

I had feared losing Giovanni – and I had lost him – that time I watched him walking off in the mountains, and I thought that it was forever. I didn't love Giovanni in the sense of desire, but I needed him. That was love too.

During our first time apart after our wedding, when he left for Turin and would be coming back the day after next or in a few days, I sank into a kind of desperation, I floundered as though I was about to drown. As though – without him – I could not breathe.

> Through the trees,
> You walk off
> (…)

In Turin he lived in a very uncomfortable family boarding house; he slept close to a kitchen that exuded the smell of garlic, which he abhorred. But I rioted more against his being far away than against his discomforts, which he glossed over. And yet I knew his extreme sensitivity, how much the mere suspicion of uncleanliness made him suffer. Instead, he told me little stories about the landladies, two friends with perhaps adventurous pasts, generous, cheerful, anything but practical; of a small, cute maid who was a tad stupid; of the invariably strange pensioners. A young woman, probably crazy, always stayed locked in her room, and only came out onto the stairs now and then to yell: she called out her husband's name – who was at work in some office – then locked herself away again. To me it seemed a menagerie out of Dostoevsky.

6

I had approached the old doctor first, for a gynaecologic exam, which turned into a 'delicate' amorous assault. Feeling embarrassed more than anything, I didn't protest, but I got dressed again in silence, a fact that seemed to offend him: I should have been grateful. I didn't tell Innocenzo about this ordeal; the old man stayed our doctor, especially since we were always healthy to begin with. I found out from my mother that he'd been a friend of my doctor uncle, who was known for being a libertine and whom the ladies liked a lot. He examined Innocenzo because of some back pain and diagnosed appendicitis; he suggested his son as a surgeon.

The operation was long and difficult; what followed was the torture of going without water, as was common then. Innocenzo had to let his facial hair grow out and I found he looked beautiful. I drew many pictures of his profile, become ascetic and sentimental.

I was so happy that I flirted (alas) not only with Innocenzo, but also with the surgeon: who wasn't a ladies' man, but attractive. I even went so far as to wear an oleander flower behind my ear. Innocenzo pointed out with his wry-indulgent smile: 'The doctor was moved!' In fact, he even invited me to watch an operation, for which he'd get me the necessary permission.

7

The bank, that mother, I never loved her, before; I didn't hate her either: it was work, nothing more. I used to like repeating the joke 'What's worse than robbing a bank?' et cetera; but he, who loved Brecht, never laughed at this line. It's also true that I never managed to grasp the concept (of a bank). Only in Singapore, when I saw the fantastic building for Mao's bank, did I surrender: to the universal, and therefore to the necessary.

I have to list the bank among his maladies: only, obviously, as a very probable cause, given the concurrences which even he reluctantly, silently acknowledged. He never complained about those painful spells; arising in his dry and healthy body, they had something unreal about them. I heard him say, as years passed, that he'd look at the enormous wheels of trucks and feel like sticking his head under. I saw him, at night, blindly wandering around the house, his head in his hands. I felt horror for that torment, and I would have liked to share in it; but I couldn't hold out for long, would plunge back into sleep. I'd remember Eugenia, who slept during Adolfo's asthma attacks at Tetto Murato: it helped me absolve myself. Behind his suffering, I glimpse the spectre of my own inattention, perhaps my flight from pain.

Over time I ended up grasping a rhythm in that persecution, numbers. A number has more to do with magic than with exact sciences. With the magic that is in nature. His crises were seasonal: four per year, but they could last a month or more. They didn't interrupt his professional life. It was monstrous; but was it also fated?

8

A malady that could have been fatal struck him while he was far away, during an extraordinary months-long stay in Peru. Why extraordinary? First of all because Peru is, still is; and extraordinary were his emotions: intense, passionate. He didn't want me to hear about his illness, I found out only when he returned; but he wrote to me of his experiences. His compassion for the indigenous people, misunderstood and in practically subhuman conditions; and an extraordinary sight: the cormorants going to the beach to die.

Those that prepare themselves to die seem, among living beings, endowed with a gift for knowing: not to all is it granted, nor is it asked. It's connected not only to a particular nature, but also to certain traditions. His friend Palma, in Singapore, brought us to see a street that was about to disappear: Sago Lane. Some traditions aren't understood any more and, unbecoming, get erased by the powers that be. Sago Lane was where old people would move when they were going to die. It was a short street, of tall, dilapidated houses. I saw a Chinese spectre in a window, standing there, motionless; maybe indeed waiting.

9

There are people who seem to have a 'calling for death', as others do for art or religion or politics. Not him (and not me either). He had, on the other hand, great pity for those who had to die.

For Silvia, one knew – no doubt she knew too – that there was no hope. Innocenzo sent her – for their wedding anniversary – an enormous yet light, upward-soaring floral arrangement: turquoise and pale pink, the way she liked them. I wouldn't have dared. He also wrote words of reassurance, expectation, and did so naturally. I didn't understand. She was happy about it and seemed as though she had truly received reassurance; and yet she was neither ignorant nor naive.

Then from London (Innocenzo's holiday) I called her every morning out of his generosity. When we returned, it was almost the end. They had told her it was bronchitis, but the young doctor said as he walked in: 'So where is this pneumonia?' Thus, she knew. I didn't know; but when she gave me her hand, small and thin – her pinkie a bit arched – with slight pressure, I felt I understood. She died during the night and I knew what she'd wanted to tell me with that slight but firm clasp of the hand.

From him, too, I received that light clasp of the hand for a while, until the fatal Sunday (of his agony).

Innocenzo never accepted that we no longer had Silvia (and then Mario). He'd say: 'I just can't.' On trips, they followed behind us, and every so often I'd ask Innocenzo, who could see them in the rearview mirror: 'Baj sequuntur?'

Silvia was happy to discover uncommon places, rare beauties in art and scenery; Mario admired (like me) the selection of good restaurants, and respect for punctuality. How beautiful those journeys were, led by Innocenzo. On the last one, they went ahead of us.

10

He read *Sons and Lovers*, after Mamma had died, and he said to me: 'Don't read it.' I'd read it many years before, I didn't understand the warning. And so it was terrible. I, too, had been gripped by a passion for my dying mother. Lawrence says something about the beauty of her eyes, and how it seemed to him that she was dying because of that; as I say in *The Guest* that maybe she was dying for the delicateness of her wrists. Innocenzo understood not only the solitude of the dying, but also of those who remain.

When he read the manuscript of *The Penumbra*, I saw that he was very sad, and when he finished reading he was on the verge of tears. He mourned, however, not their death, but the end of the narration. He said: 'You love these two extraordinary people, and you lose them with the end of the book. You sense that we won't see them again.' (He saw them again in a dream.)

When Papà died, I was overcome by the memory of his gentle, incredibly good nature; but his melancholic, silent old age had already distanced me from him. Emotionally I was far away. And who he really was, I've understood it now, through his rediscovered photos from Demonte. Just as I've understood truly what his wife – my mother – was to him.

When he died, he was very old and tired. He looked at her awhile, intensely, then he closed his eyes. That look was nostalgia, gratitude, and still love.

11

Innocenzo understood my attachment to my past loves. When Giovanni underwent an operation for a potentially fatal illness, he sent me to visit him in Sanremo. Just as he had me brought to Turin to say goodbye to dying Anthony.

My relationship with Anthony is all in the poem 'We went lightly', and in a few other similar poems, which express the impossibility of that love.

In the hospital, I at the foot of the bed, Renata next to the headboard. She asked: 'Do you come to Turin often?' 'Rarely, but I always like it.' 'What do you like?' 'The avenues…'

Then he, the sheet pulled up to his chin, slid out his hand and gave me 'that' wave. The hand from back then, unreal and far off like the moon; the hand now, weighed down, as if already of the earth, itself earth. But real.

12

Luciana reminded me of a visit to the Villar cemetery. Again I saw that bright morning, Maria's large family tomb: during those visits I always think of their houses which are so poor, the patched and darned curtains, a single cow in the shed, and then that rich tomb. There was a picture of her, wearing glasses, like a knowing (even comical) old lady. Innocenzo read the tombstones; Maria's sister-in-law Laide had died just a few days – maybe one day – after her husband. He commented: 'How lucky they were!' He said this seriously; actually, wistfully.

Who knows how many times I had made this silly remark: 'Luckily, I'm older (by three years): I'll die first.' It was selfishness, naturally.

Once – he didn't repeat himself – he told me he had 'chosen', that is hoped to die first: since life gets privileged over death; but then – that 'then' means living, evaluating his responsibilities and above all considering what was best for me – he had 'chosen' to die second. So that I wouldn't miss him.

For me, the privilege of dying with him by my side was simply not to be.

13

After I had lost him, they said to me, when talking or in letters: 'I know you feel cold.' But I wrote this sentence (for no one, to myself): 'I am not cold. I am still wrapped in the rough wool of his sweetness.'

I'd always been alone, in the sense of free. But with him all moments, sensations, smells, contact, words, silences, were imbued with love.

Many years before a famous film distorted the meaning of the expression, making it a cliché about high society, I had called ours a *dolce vita*, a sweet life: in a secret poem, written in the canzonet form. The only person who read it – a poet – deemed it Goethean. (Which means: it seems stupid, but it's perfect.)

> Of nights, love, our
> sweet life is made.
> We break the endless
> chain of useless days,
> and lonely boredom
> from embraces cast,
> reborn is joy
> in us to last.

There is no desiring among the dead; but I am still alive. I was struck by what Simone de Beauvoir said when she was old: 'le désir mort'. So it was she who was dead.

14

I've been reading Moravia's *The Voyeur*: in it they love each other by using special, systematic techniques; we, if anything, did things – spontaneously – because we loved each other. On p. 186, the noises: 'sweet, sweet moans from her; from him, the actual sound of a wild beast'. Us, the opposite.

In Duras (*L'Amant*): 'la jouissance qui fait crier'. I had not expected this from sex. I considered my first orgasms his doing. He was what made me feel 'la jouissance'. I judged it his task, and his merit.

It was beautiful to climax with someone who didn't seem hedonistic, but knowledgeable. *How* could he have been? He had never visited brothels, or ladies. It always seemed indiscreet – even for me – to ask. It must be that in this, too, one is born mature. ('Mature men are born,' was an aphorism of Pavese's.)

I used to think of us: he, something dry, warm, hard, and yet also soft. Myself, something damp, ardent, and yet also 'stony'. I said it in a poem:

> no one can rob us of joy
> our subterranean joy
> like softest water
> like a vein in stone

15

In Paris, in a brasserie, with Itala and Antonio. I asked: 'Why did you two get married?' Her response: 'I wanted a lover, not a husband.' Same for me; except I hadn't formulated it like that to myself. I've always hated the words: wife, husband, and also lover (the roles); and why no intolerance for father, mother, son? Because it's sex which, officialized, becomes ridiculous, awkward, embarrassing.

That time with Eva and Luigi at the Soldato, talking about 'separate rooms'. I didn't suspect the drama they were going through (her suicide was already imminent) and said: 'I got married to sleep with him.' Eva smiled: painfully (I understood later).

I had noticed, as a little girl, that old couples slept in separate beds, if not in different rooms (even Grandpa and Grandma at Tetto Coppi).

In these last few years, in hotels, we always asked for separate beds and I was amused that they must have found it natural for old people like us, who instead still loved each other. We slept apart for our different tastes in covers, for my own frustration: he'd always end up throwing off the bedsheet, and wrapping himself in the covers.

The last cloth I wrapped him in, too, was not a sheet, but a plaid blanket.

16

I continued to think of him – I still think of him? – as my possession. In the sense of 'no one else's'.

I shouted (in the act of possession): 'You're mine! You're mine!' with jealous passion. Final year, final months.

A poem – perhaps the first one that was 'ours':

> the naughty girl
> who cruelly shouted at you: you're mine!
> I am her, too.

That little girl, the daughter of a marshal from the barracks where they would play, had grabbed his infantile sex, shouting those words. The whole poem is powerful: I identified with all of them:

> that girl who chose your books
> with loving friendship
> (...)
> the one who bathed
> her letters in tears.

Really, I was always not exactly jealous, but disdainful of the others. My identifying with them in that poem was an act of humility, at heart. I felt jealous only towards the last one, and passion was, at least for him, not even there; but for her as well. An imaginary thing, yet existing on a noble, chaste level.

17

My jealousy towards that 'last one' began one evening when I arrived late to the clinic – the operation had been serious – because I'd thought I needed to go to a talk given by Maria Corti; I then immediately ran off at the end, thus accumulating my mistakes. I enter the room out of breath, and I see two smiles: he with his head on the pillow, and she spoon-feeding him. Those smiles seemed happy to me.

Maybe it was the year before his fatal malady; perhaps I was already in a state of alarm – unknowingly – for this real thing, and I thought I was for this imaginary one: it's possible.

A while after that, in a moment of normal life, I had a relapse, and this time too for a small act of kindness. The woman had sent a cake she'd baked herself; since it was hard, undercooked, I only tasted it. He ate all of it, a little at a time, of course: chewing slowly, 'with compunction', I thought. It was proof of his excessive attachment.

The lowest point of my wretchedness – but it was also of my helplessness – was when he spoke to her for a long time on the phone one evening. Maybe she had come back from summer holiday and he was updating her. But I thought: if I can manage to convince myself that he's not 'all mine', I'll suffer less.

Passion is selfish, after all. But I had come to this because now I was afraid: of being unable to bear it.

18

Once he told me that he 'didn't see' ugly women. Maybe he didn't want to see them, like when Piero as a little boy would close his eyes to not see Martina in Turin.

Or he only meant that he *saw* beautiful women. (I remembered the Futurists' claim: 'Humanity is divided into: beautiful women – men and ugly women.')

He had a special way of saying 'beautiful', with a closed *u* sound. The description often began with 'as tall as me'. This line thrilled me: 'You use yourself as a paragon of beauty!'

It was much more subtle than that.

I see again the grateful smile, the joy of that miserable colleague of mine (thin, pale, minute) when I told her that he had defined her as 'a woman'. We'd run into her on the street, and I'd said hello. 'How did she come across to you,' I'd asked, 'ugly, pretty?' He'd replied: 'She's a woman.' She understood and was pleased by it.

19

He had a childhood love, in Este. In the first year of middle school: a little blonde girl, from the first row. For her he had agreed to perform in *Scapin the Schemer*, and even in the dialogue *What You Learn Dusting*, in which she (in the role of his sister) was the protagonist, and he a supporting actor. It was truly a great love; he had to overcome a deep aversion. Nothing was as alien to him as the work of an actor: for him it was actually incomprehensible that someone could choose to practise that craft. He felt a kind of moral horror towards it: coming out of oneself! And yet he loved going to the theatre, not only reading plays, and he admired actors, including in film.

I think it was fear: of being violated. It recalled the terror he'd felt at the circus, as a child, when the clown sat next to him.

He brought little Andreina to the theatre, where there was a children's show; they invited them to go on stage, and Andreina immediately ran up. He felt the old fear, in her place; and Andreina herself seemed different to him, alien.

20

Another love was the little Jewish girl in Perugia. I see again, from his stories, a small courtyard with a few flowerbeds, in that little neighbourhood perched on a spur called Porta Sole (is there, in Perugia, a Porta Sole?), and their easy, hushed games. His mother grew worried 'because she was Jewish', and she brought it up with Father Anselmo. The friar, a great friend and protector of young Innocenzo, was appalled and approved the friendship. The girl was named Nissim. That name used to come up in radio broadcasts; I wanted him to look into it: the little girl from long ago had a brother who studied music, as a matter of fact. But he would shake his head.

And he hadn't wanted to for the girl from Tortona, either. She was quite young, like him. He had met her on an uphill road: maybe going to his uncle's villa, by the castle? She was holding a pack of charcoal, which had ripped; the charcoal had scattered on the ground, and he helped her pick it up.

When he left again after his holiday, she went to say goodbye to him at the station; his grandfather understood and gave them some privacy. They wrote to each other, maybe only postcards, I'm not sure. I always wanted to incorporate those stories, those people – somewhat absurdly – as my own. He never knew what became of her, and he wouldn't have wanted to. Maybe because she truly had mattered to him a great deal.

21

I found a letter from the woman from Montevideo; and why don't I write to her? Maybe she knows by now. I don't feel like writing, I'd prefer to see her or speak on the phone. I met her – I don't think she knew who I was – in the corridor of a train. Her face, calm and beautiful, was tragic. I knew that she was getting married and would be going to South America. Her face was oval, white; oval, too, her light blue eyes. I felt an attraction towards her, even a kind of love. Now there is also the allure of the word 'Montevideo', of that sound and that remoteness.

Like that other name – not of the woman, nor of a city, but of a street in Milan. The woman on Viale Tunisia. I believe she was French. She personified his ideal in terms of feminine beauty. She was tall and slender, her hair ash blonde, flowing. She played the piano. An Odette? Rather, she was a 'true lady'. For me she was unreal: the only thing tangible is 'Viale Tunisia'.

Perhaps he didn't speak to me of her enough? I've always been a horrible listener, and on top of that there was my scarce patience (for women). He didn't give me 'updates' on women who liked him, much less on the ones who – especially towards the end – 'offered themselves'. I looked down on them from the start; I don't believe he did, he was much more humane. The ones about whom he talked to me a little, I didn't look down on, because it was a sign that he thought highly of them.

22

His two friends from the bank – friends not because they were similar to him, but for their singularity. Bizarre, innocent, generous. One, above all, because he was a simple man, the second, a free spirit. The 'free' one was named Jencek. He hailed from Trieste and had a very Central European appearance, Hungarian for me. He played the violin like a virtuoso, tzigane style. One winter night, in Trieste, after playing in an orchestra, he bet that he could swim across the port – fully dressed – and he did. Another time, once again for a bet, he drank a bottle of alcohol in one go, grappa or cognac.

Other, more beautiful stories concerned his civil courage during Fascism, his scrupulousness coupled with his complete lack of enthusiasm at the bank. His wife – his second or third – was a very refined woman from Turin. He first caught sight of her in Turin, in fact, where she was a seamstress with a willowy profile. She always had a headache, because she worked in a basement. He went to report the shop owner. It was a high-end shop which counted a royal princess among its clients. There were consequences that I don't recall.

23

Ingarao's first name was Carmelo, 'like all Sicilians'. A Sicilian from Syracuse, the kind they call 'babbi' – dopes. In Turin they referred to him as 'Baron Ingarao' because he always dressed in black. He was a sort of double of Vittorini, a comical, blundering, and yet similar-looking alter ego. They were friends as boys, classmates, had played together in the legendary train station of Elio's father. At school Elio did his composition assignments for him, and he Elio's maths homework. But Vittorini said he didn't remember him.

Innocenzo said that Ingarao was unable to write a letter without making a few errors in grammar or syntax. For me, my enchanted vision of Syracuse also comprises his poetic figure, ingenuous and gentlemanly.

The first time, we went to root him out in the bank, where his desk was at the top of a stairwell, a kind of landing. His devotion to Innocenzo was full of happiness.

He had an extremely shy sister, dressed in black, whom he lived with. His letters always included greetings to me from this sister, who couldn't manage to open her mouth whenever we met. Now he is dead; she wrote me a long letter, and says that her brother left this world 'on tiptoes like a saint'.

24

There was also that more senior, old-fashioned colleague (he was from Bergamo) who served somewhat as a model for my *Man Who Talked Alone*. They were in an office together, under a central manager who was a bit of a lowlife. They were hard years. 'They'll say we did our work together,' quipped this colleague, who had a certain sense of humour. One would go – myself included – to the Biffi Scala on Sunday mornings (they had to work on Sundays too). The excursions with our skis were over!

This colleague was named Luigi and he had a lovely surname, which had belonged to an actor: Carminati. Since he had a striking profile, Innocenzo convinced him to get rid of the floppy hat that he wore down over his neck and which made him look like a peasant; he went with him to buy a light grey hat with a raised brim, which had him resembling a lord. He was a delicate man, but unread. Innocenzo tried to convert him. He didn't succeed; he had attempted with his father too, to no avail. The Colonel, like Mr Carminati, read the illustrated Sunday supplement, *La Domenica del Corriere*.

I found Innocenzo's pedagogical vein naive, though noble. Similarly, in Parma he'd bring everyone, foreigners and Italians alike, to see the Cathedral and the Baptistry, his great passion. I could imagine with what results.

25

We detected a mouse, in our home on Via Signorelli. We'd come across tiny tracks, nibbled paper. Innocenzo was the one who ended up finding it (Piero and I, I imagine, were on vacation). He discovered the mouse's provisions behind the bookcase in the hallway, a little pile of potatoes. It was moving; but when he spotted the mouse, he came at it with a broom. He missed and then realized it had taken refuge in the laundry basket; it stayed there, covered by a towel, and he could see its behind trembling. He brandished the broom again, but a laughing fit came over him; he didn't strike it. He took pity on it.

Pity is fundamental. How he liked that line of Shakespeare's in *Othello*: 'and I loved her that she did pity them'.

And I loved him that he did pity: not me, even if in his way of loving me there was surely compassion, and therefore pity. I intuited it; now I know it.

He felt pity for his enemies. He didn't have enemies: I mean for people he very well could have detested. He *saw* meanness, it repulsed him, but if it was directed at him, he ignored it.

With Enzo Paci – not only in the old Cuneo stories when he'd been truly wronged by him (as I found out later), but also in their many years of friendship in Milan, laced with a certain superciliousness on the part of the philosopher – he managed before me to recognize traces of naiveté, fragility, in that successful man.

Then when he was sick, neurotic (he suffered from a persecution complex) and felt abandoned one tragic summer – his wife called us – Innocenzo listened to him, subtly comforted him, gave him practical advice, clarification. In short, he took pity.

26

There's no pity without humour. This humour must be scorching.

In the fifties we'd go to Camogli with Luigi, Eva and a friend of theirs, a dentist. We stayed at the Drin, in Punta Chiappa. That man, the dentist, was passionate about fishing. He was equipped with all the tools, implements: nets, rods, traps, and he even had a motor boat at his disposal. Not that he ever caught a fish, despite busying himself and tinkering around endlessly. Innocenzo called him 'the abstract fisherman'.

Bacchelli was very amusing, whenever he'd talk about his family back home (it happened rarely). A few stories revolved around an uncle whom he called 'my jackass uncle', a simpleton in his very learned family. In that famous writer – though now forgotten while still alive – Innocenzo picked up hints of naive vanity (vanity almost always is) and once said: '*He's* the jackass uncle.'

Humour is more subtle when it alludes to something essential, to an important choice. He thus defined an affinity of his, in the realm of history, politics and morals, which matured throughout his life: 'They tell me I don't love my country. I do love it, actually. Only that my country is England.'

27

When I was asked to choose a virtue, as the topic of a 'conversation', I wanted to propose Disdain. He instead suggested Indifference. Like 'unconcern' (Galileo). I wondered how many times he must have affirmed it inside himself: to have it so ready.

I don't know the secret workings of his inner language; however, it's true that now almost everyone seems mediocre, or at least limited.

He was incisive, but he could gloss over things. Where he found amusement, he referenced – often – the 'professor', the brother-in-law from *Uncle Vanya*.

We had a little model, exclusive to us. We were eating at the crowded Baita del Sole in Pila. Between the tables, a little boy – beautiful, for that matter – planted himself in front of another, smaller (younger) boy, stuck two thumbs under his trouser braces and asked: 'What school are you in?' The other boy looked at him perplexed; the first one declared: 'I'm in second nursery.' Evidently there are grades in nursery school too; and so the minuscule scene truly gets to the heart of all academic vanity.

Indifference was meant to be a medicine for me. I had recounted dreams before anyone else and revealed their *poésie naturelle*; then with my 'simple heart' I had written a 'blade of grass' novel, the way Flaubert liked; and then the 'Resistance without the Resistance': an intimist Resistance, the sole possible kind if one doesn't adopt the epic scope of Fenoglio; and on and on.

He knew that I'm not unaware of the value of my writing. And whenever the wild beast inside me growled, he'd say: 'Remember how Cervantes suffered in Lope de Vega's shadow!' He truly thought it was a valid comparison, insofar as my work didn't receive adequate recognition precisely for its intrinsic superiority. 'Remember Lope de Vega!'

28

Not only a need for justice was behind his choices (in politics), but pity once again. His faith in good peoples (the Russians). His understanding-compassion for the poor, who are no longer such in the old sense of the term, they have social protections, et cetera; but...

Arriving one morning, Rachele said – somewhat haughtily – that a woman (namely, another maid) had advised her to get paid by the hour. It was in her best interests, she said. Innocenzo did the calculations on a sheet of paper and in the end he explained to her that, in this way, he'd have to not pay for the hours she didn't work. She got frightened and again chose the comprehensive method (I don't know what it's called). I felt a little indignant; but he said: 'You know, they always have to ask...'

29

Indignation is noble; not anger. Anger manifested itself in him through pallor. He'd force it down. But by the violence that follows from rage, he felt tempted.

The most extraordinary instance goes back to his childhood. His mother had taken him to nursery school. The drama began when they started to slip the little smock on him. He refused with such determination, his mother had to surrender, take him back home. The reason for his anger is interesting: he thought the smock would make him equivalent to a little girl. It's quite funny; but this, let's say sexual element in the story isn't what matters, here. It's instead another detail. While his mother and the nun were trying to reason with his stubbornness, he stared at – it was at eye-level for him – a pair of enormous scissors dangling by the nun's stomach, and his exact impulse was this: stick those scissors in that belly. It's no longer all that funny.

In Cuneo his mother had gone, all smiles, to the bank to sell tickets for a charity raffle. I could understand his irritation, his anger; but he, in his retelling, said: 'I felt like strangling her.'

At this point I understood that his pallor – in that first and only visit of mine to the bank – which I flattered myself into thinking was the overwhelming emotion of love, was rage. For the intrusion, for the violence of frivolity in his own secret prison.

30

Did I ever have anything to hold against him? Two obscure points, one very small, the other big. The first, when we were 'engaged'. He had looked at his watch – or at least so it seemed to me – while embracing me (in the living room in Cuneo). Was he bored? I never asked him. And how could I have? If he was, it was a brief interval; and besides, he had a completely natural way about him. Actually, this was also his charm, because it was the naturalness of a poet, gratuitous, unpredictable and yet sure, in a certain sense rational. He did not *perform* passion, and I knew this. He didn't use the verb to love, other than – maybe – in letters (but I don't think so). What I want to say is this: his style, that is his language, was similar to mine in writing: concrete for sensations, reticent with facts, secretive but not duplicitous in feelings.

31

Now for that other thing. He hadn't been there when I gave birth.

During the night I felt pain coming in waves. I called out to him, I shook him. His sleep – like that night with the burglars, when he'd fallen asleep by the window – transformed him into a dead man. Warm, fragrant, but heavy, unmovable. Since the pain was intermittent, I wasn't truly afraid. When I succeeded in waking him, he disappeared and came back with my mother (ghostly pale) and the midwife. Immediately he left again. (I see him, waving a hand, as he slips into the hallway.) And so, during the procedure – I was about to say the ceremony – he wasn't there, he had gone to the bank. It didn't upset me at all, then. I must have also thought that that was the way things were done, but most of all I wouldn't have wanted him to see me in such a state. Who knows why I even rubbed it in his face later, at least I fear I did. But that must have been after our philosopher friend Turin boasted of having been at his wife's side the times she gave birth. I know very well that Innocenzo did not stay firstly for his horror of blood, then out of modesty and, finally, respect.

32

In terms of the birth, I later thought that it was out of modesty but also fear. I recalled his fear when I realized that Piero, in his father's last days, frequently came to see him, but would leave again right away. The nurse told me that males always do that. With my quickness in catching doubles, I immediately connected this desertion of Piero's with Innocenzo's all those years ago during his birth. I then concluded, in both cases, out of 'respect'. It's a somewhat antiquated concept, now, but a valid one. I said to Piero, after his death: 'You should have taken a photograph of your dad in these final days.' He replied: 'I thought about it, but it would have shown a lack of respect towards him.' Marvellous Piero.

33

I eventually connected his repulsion for transfusions – which transpired only from an ironic sigh or two – with his repulsion for raw or undercooked meat, with blood. It seemed to me that his disgust and his inability to bear dirtiness were also of the same nature.

I always washed myself less than he did (at the very least, a daily bath and shower for him). I'd ask him: 'And me? Do I not bathe enough?' 'But you'd never know,' he'd admit, unironically.

In the 'bodily' we were different, opposites. For this and in spite of this, there was that constant (erotic) chemistry between us – alive, never tiring. The correspondence between bodies, call it eros or love, is mysterious. And, like every material virtue, symbolic.

34

The image that perhaps says everything about him, the one I never tired of looking at, is an image of elegance; but I prefer to say of style. The crescent shape – gothic, or Chinese too – of his body in the Legion of Honour photo (one of many). His head in profile, tilted slightly back as though looking at something from above. A smile just hinted at – wry, indulgent – lips sealed. As if he were thinking: Why yes, they're good... He would look that way at two children or two cats playing. An archaic smile.

When I was in high school, my parents had gone to Turin to see the Biennial at the Promotrice. They brought me back the catalogue and Mamma showed me the painting she'd liked the most. A young, tall man looks pensively at a lake; an overcoat folded on his arm, he's seen from below, almost from behind. It was titled *The Poet*. At the time I preferred a fearsome De Chirico self-portrait; but I didn't forget that image in which I later identified Innocenzo. I consider it one of my premonitions of him, of his happening.

35

Casorati said about him: 'Lalla's husband is beautiful, sentimental. He has sad eyes.' I knew it; he wasn't sure that I was truly loved by my friends in Turin.

In my books Innocenzo is a virile character: rational, a protector; but he was also feminine: gentle, fanciful. Such that his face's 'manly' beauty was not aggressive, but delicate, in its strong structure. That strength was granted by the prominence of his cheekbones: the 'nomad' structure (which I'd first discovered with Giovanni and which I always need). And manly beauty is more complete if it has something feminine. As with the spirit, in fact.

For me, his particular, infinitely contemplated beauty – going back forever – was his sleeping face. He was Saint Orsola sleeping with a cheek propped against her hand (Carpaccio, in the Gallerie in Venice). That was his flair when it came to sleep.

This – rare – character of strength and sweetness, I find it again in other paintings as well. In Giorgione's *Young Man*, in which the sweetness is accentuated by his long, loose hair, and also in Courbet's *Self-Portrait*.

36

I teased him because for a beautiful woman he said 'as tall as me'. The teasing was for that 'as me'; however, it was only logical, because I felt how objective his definition was, as though he were speaking of a painting. He said *beautiful* savouring the word, and more often said 'very beautiful', emphasizing the *very*. I thought he exaggerated sometimes, like any man, for feminine beauty; but he also said it that way for men, for children, for animals. I liked his wonder, actually, his astonishment at beauty. In describing it, the words swelled, its expression was ecstatic.

One woman he'd loved in a painting was a Correggio (he had a copy of it in his office in Parma). She resembled me, he said, in the nude. But also women in paintings who didn't resemble me at all. Like that stern Flemish woman with the tall, stiff veil held in place with a pin, or Cranach's playful *Venus*.

37

So, physical modesty in him wasn't out of disdain for the body, but respect. And the last days were also an affirmation of this. As they were of his repulsion for dirtiness. I always had the impression that he bathed not to clean himself but as an act of worship. I had fun watching him, and always laughed when he'd flour his sweet and robust ornaments with talcum powder, turning them over as one does in the kitchen with things to fry.

When it came to the sun, too, we were different. In the mountains, he always positioned himself with his face in the sunlight, I in the shade. He Nordic, I Eastern. 'Are you taking in the sun to get a tan?' I'd say, making fun of him (I don't understand the general obsession with tanning). In the winter he'd rub snow on his face, before going into the sunlight. He'd turn golden, not red. I liked that we seemed, in colours too, a man and a woman like in archaic paintings.

38

Did I have it, the 'wild life'? The one I'd desired while looking at him, at the Pagarì cabin?

I was, my nature is – I don't know whether in my core or where – wild.

I would rattle him, with my shouted sneezes: he'd give a pained start. My laugh was that way too when I was young; but that didn't bother him. Only in England would he suggest I lower my voice, in restaurants (I noticed that it was the English, of all people, who laughed loudly if they were in a group). My laughs really amused the maids: not my Maria, aristocratic and in any event respectful, but the ones back home, at my grandparents'. I believe they loved me for this.

But I was wild in my relationship to food, too. My preference for raw or undercooked meat; the heads of birds, of fish, the bones to suck on, to break between my teeth. With a slightly wicked smile he admitted that his mother, too, liked 'the heads': the sole common trait between us.

In London we celebrated many of our wedding anniversaries (the 20th of August). He would always offer me the grouse, which is served only in those days, after the 17th. My grouse was bloody, and it had to be so.

These things have a strong symbolic value, they are something that resides in one's entire being, not only in the body:

> the ancient baying replies,
> not from solitary roads,
> from the soul's naked fields.

39

If there was one common trait between my mother-in-law and me (eating heads, feet), there must have been others too; I always doubted as much. She was a guileless woman of extreme sincerity, energetic and brave. Orphaned as a child, she was educated at the Army Daughters boarding school in Turin. She was much more 'military' than the Colonel.

During the Great War she left her father-in-law's home (the grandfather from Tortona) and joined her husband in the zone behind the front. They lived in a room on the ground floor of some seamstresses; they slept all together, she, Innocenzo and the two little girls, in a big bed. In the evening he would shut the door and the windows himself, fastening them with planks; then he'd accompany the girls to the bathroom which was in the courtyard, with a candle. He was in elementary school and his report cards bore the Emperor's coat of arms with the two-headed eagle. Their teacher brought the students to visit the soldiers. They saw the chaotic flight from Caporetto, in the rain. They managed to get on a train; Innocenzo was pushed onto a train car, his mother onto another; he held the two little girls' hands.

In his last days he thought back on that period of time. He said: 'My father told me that when we die, we see ourselves as children again.' He'd smile at the memory of eating snacks in the meadows, with his mother and baby sisters. Who knows, maybe it was a little bit 'the wild life'.

When they were in Perugia, she allowed him to go on long walks, for a couple of days even, in those hills with a companion.

She was strict, but she trusted him. A little story amused me a great deal. He had to get a notebook from a friend who lived in a working-class neighbourhood; the boy's mother asked him, 'Who are you?' He remembered an instruction his mother had given him and replied, 'I'm the son of the Captain of the Carabinieri.' The woman shouted: 'We've never had any business with the Carabinieri!'

I also liked it because it was the 'double' of a family story. My grandmother would instruct my aunts: 'Always say you're the nieces of your priest uncle!'

40

I was certainly the person least like his mother Innocenzo could have found. When the marriage was agreed upon, she said to my mother that a countess friend of hers had advised her against accepting a schoolteacher as a daughter-in-law. Mamma hadn't said anything in response, had feared for me. In fact, after we were married my mother-in-law immediately came to inspect the house, the drawers (I found out from Maria). It didn't happen a second time, Innocenzo must have dissuaded her. Then, getting older, she did love me, and I grew fond of her too; I liked her, actually.

Not only my mother-in-law, but almost all the women who knew him deplored the fact that he'd married me. But he didn't love housewives, the ones who have a vocation for it, I mean. He wouldn't have been able to bear a protective wife. He'd recall with horror how his mother would accompany her husband to the tailor when he needed to have civilian clothes made.

41

Innocenzo in his family home is revealed by a dream of his that I recounted in *The Metamorphoses*. It's titled 'The Other'.

'I must have gone back to being a boy. We're living in a barracks like when my father was in the service. I do my schoolwork sitting at a little table in the barracks courtyard. Next to me a carabiniere cleans his rifle. They call me from our home. They send me out to look for "the other": I don't know if he's my brother, they've never told me. He's identical to me in everything; my height, dressed like me. Rarely are we able to see him; he's a rebel, almost always out of the house. They send me to look for him because only I know where he is. The barracks are built on the slope of an arid and rocky mountain overlooking the sea. It's an ancient sea, crisscrossed by sailboats, with an intense colour. I find the other sitting as always on a rock, looking off into the distance. As soon as he sees me, he walks towards me smiling, and we head back inland together. He shares with me that this time he's going to run away; he leaves me a book written in English, telling me to translate it. It's his story: that of a boy who runs away from home because he can't stand his family, the conversations at the dinner table. I've made it to page seven. My parents have noticed that the other hasn't come back inside; they order me to go look for him. I say that it's pointless, that he won't be coming back this time. I do my best to convince them: "Don't try to make him come back, you'd only lose him. If someone goes, in some way he stays; if you forced him to return, you'd lose him forever." They don't understand; they insist that I go look for him and bring him back home. I pretend to obey and I go up the mountain. At the usual spot, on a bench (…).'

The story doesn't end there, but I'll stop. It's enough.

42

As a little boy, on the school walk – in that little village behind the front – he carried the flag for the whole day without ever peeing, so he wouldn't have to ask for permission. Modesty takes away certain joys but enhances others.

When we were 'engaged' we'd go entire days without peeing; and intimacy never led to true indifference. That Frenchman who defined a wife as someone in front of whom 'on peut péter' said something profound if it's restricted to necessity.

He told me of his own inability, when he was with men who were all pissing together and chatting, and he simply couldn't.

If I was sometimes reluctant towards this kind of intimacy, it wasn't out of modesty, at least not in the sense of dignity, but savage resistance – the reverse expression of going wild. I believe he meant this when he wrote to me 'you will never be old'.

43

Every moment from his childhood was big in some way. Because of his awareness, I think.

There was first of all the gruesome image of a headless goose running around like mad. There were also the chickens, which his mother strangled in bed when she was sick, because her military husband preferred not to. But this was comedic (domestic).

The first real discovery of death was painful, tragic. He was just a little boy; running in the grass, he stepped on a chick. While he told the story, compassionately he relived his horror. He never shook off that sense of guilt. It was the mysterious remorse of unintended harm.

For the third story I can say that I lived it, because I saw it (in his telling). There is the vastness of a wide landscape – not unsettling. It's a summer afternoon, kids after gym class sit on the steps of a church, by a sunny road outside Perugia. He leans his shoulders against the closed church door. The door gives way, opens a little. Inside, in the darkness, an old man lies stretched out on the floor. Dead. His face emaciated, his grey facial hair grown out, his eyes glassy. In his memory he'd made his peace with it; he had seen himself, without recognizing himself: innocently, without fear.

44

With his aversion to being an actor, his knack for portraying himself became accentuated. Count Lanza: 'The personification of a Piedmontese gentleman.' Mrs Abbozzo: 'An exquisite man.'

In general meetings he always took a seat at the back (he was entitled to the front). Me: 'That's an ostentatious display too, but backwards.' Maurizio Mattioli, who was present: 'No, everyone understands.'

What did they understand? They understood the meaning. I believe I hadn't understood right away because it had to do with the 'world of men'. But then I was illuminated. Everyone understood because *it came from him*.

After little Luciana's old, playful character assessment, practical prudent resolute (like Cavour), which I imagine perfectly fits what he was like as a working man, the most beautiful assessment was that of Mattioli (Raffaele), as brilliant as one might expect from him. 'I'm walking down the hallway,' he said, 'and, passing in front of a door, I hear voices having an argument. I make out Innocenzo's voice. I think: Innocenzo's there, so everything is all right.'

45

At an unusual hour, he didn't come in with his key, but instead the driver rang the bell, handed me his briefcase, and disappeared. Smiling at me, he looked uncertain, sweet and a little lost, almost as if he had been drinking (an impossibility). As though apologizing, he said: 'I had an accident.' He was there, and so I didn't feel scared. A great number of problems followed that accident, though not immediately. (He was with colleagues, who'd all miraculously survived, given that the car was destroyed.)

That apology of his repeated itself almost identically, by which I mean with embarrassment, hesitation, though without him looking lost. An accident this time, too. The one with the car, caused by a driver's recklessness, was the fruit of chance; this one, more event than accident, was the now ripened fruit of his past, of his worth.

Why place the two side by side? Because there must be a reason for that repetition. The second time was once again later than usual; I was sitting in the kitchen. He came in unhurriedly – he always moved energetically, despite his sciatica – but he seemed tired; he said: 'I have news.' Me: 'Good or bad?' 'Depends on how you take it.' (Significant trait of *my* character.) He said, still standing: 'I've been named president.' My emotion was unforeseeable. It summarized a lifetime. I hugged him, sobbing. I not only don't overvalue professional positions, I ignore them. Maybe he feared I'd consider the whole thing a nuisance. What overwhelmed me was the long-carried burden of his subordinate work, of his infinite patience. I cried not out of joy, but out of pity.

I better assessed the meaning of this event (which concerned his world, extraneous to me) than the other happening, which heralded pain.

46

I know of course that what matters isn't what happens to a person, but how that person lives it. For his appointment as president: the opportunity arose and he was the 'man for the job', as they say. However, as he'd once explained to me, he was not part of the elite.

But I now want only extreme incidents. Like that time he said 'yessir' on the phone.

It was the lowest, or rather the only humiliating moment (in my opinion). Because it seems to me that he was always respected even by the biggest bastards among his superiors, during his long life going up the ranks. It's not a distant event; he was already an executive, as far as I can tell, certainly not a clerk. Why that 'servant's' word? Countless worthy men have needed to respond that way to unworthy superiors. It's phrasing that sounds servile, but it can not be; and certainly in his case it wasn't. The fact remains that it wasn't 'like him'. The only explanation would be a warpage caused by his military upbringing. Now one can perhaps find it in *belle époque* comedies, in tragedies like *Wozzeck*.

When I was in middle school, I believe we still responded that way, to our teachers. A small memory, which confirms the use of the phrase, is indeed comedic. Our teacher: 'Are you brothers?' (to one of two children with the same surname). The response: '*Nossir*, we're twins.' Here the recruit-like style is fitting.

47

All children, but especially ours who is an emblematic child, think their parents have been successful in life: to accuse them. But the best, deep down, know. And so it was with Piero, in a dream. And dreams tell the truth, about the dreamer who – as in this case – remembers the dream.

Piero tells me: 'Dad's head was bandaged, his teeth hurt and at the bank they forced him to work. And so I killed all of his bosses.' Marvellous Piero.

48

I wrote (I don't know when) this note:

'A person very advanced in years (me?), recalling moments in their life, realizes with surprise that certain behaviours of theirs in not exactly youthful years (after forty) reflected adolescent character traits.'

I truly think that drawn-out childhood and youth, with their 'innocence' guarantee a slow maturing process, and perhaps long life.

He was mature when he was young, therefore his youth was long and almost unchanging; and so it was for me, as I followed his rhythm, pressing yet *largo* (musical tempo).

I consider 'consolations': that he was old only a month; and that he did not see me old. I had always thought (felt) that we would never be ruined by age. I perhaps will be, but it no longer matters.

49

In Saint-Nicolas we found the cabin occupied, the last time. Later, I considered it an omen. For that matter, I'd thought that we wouldn't come back again, because he, as he walked ahead of me, didn't say anything, but was clearly struggling. Years earlier on the steep trail from Saint Jacques to the Pian di Verra he'd stopped every so often to wait for me; then he'd made me walk ahead so that I would be the one to set the pace. In the end I'd preferred for him to walk in front. I, who'd always been shorter of breath, now kept leaving him behind. Thinking back on it, it was something enormous, frightening; how was it possible that I didn't fully understand what it meant?

The cabin had been ours for years; it had been built to store tools, and on Sundays no one was there. It was a room with a little wooden terrace where I'd lie out to sleep after a lunch of bread and fontina cheese. Innocenzo, sitting on a board resting on two logs, would lean against the wall facing westward.

50

What was the enchantment of Saint-Nicolas? The road through the pine forest with its warm smell, one of the nicest in the world; on the sides of the road, blocks of frozen snow (it was a wintertime walk), which I kicked at until they went tumbling down. Sometimes stones, too – it had been a childhood delight. He didn't approve but he didn't scold me.

The true enchantment was after, in the light: the valley, the Emilius, the backlit Grivola, the profile of the Granta Parei at the end of the Rhêmes Valley. All this, however, was only the surrounding court: in the centre there wasn't a summit, but a col, a 'saddle'. White, because it was a glacier: the Ruitor. It always appeared to me as though it had to be passed over in flight. Like the Pillars of Hercules: for 'the beyond'. Contemplated infinite times, and always with a sense of peace. I thought of it for Silvia; then I always asked myself: and now, whose turn will it be? But it was a consoling sight, even exhilarating.

51

Already in Demonte, as a little girl, when looking from the balcony at the valley shaped like an open valve, I thought of it as a 'towards somewhere'. The vision pointing to an elsewhere was the wide col of the Madonna del Colletto (where I once saw the moon suspended in the middle, like a host).

I've had two framed images, in my study, for years. None of the Ruitor, in part because I frequently saw it again. But these have the same meaning and function. I cut one out from a newspaper. It's a landscape – I don't think I have to say symbolic, but real – of a *beyond*. It is a split iceberg: a ship passes between the two walls of ice, as though through a valley. I've always called it 'in farthest seas'.

Real, as in thought with words, but *seen* after that image and only *through* that image.

On the same wall is an image of the Valley of the Muses, cut out from the Einaudi edition of Philippson's book (Pavese told me that it was the Valley of the Muses). It is, like all of the Greece I've seen, rocky, solitary, open to the sky.

52

When did Mamma know of her death sentence? She never said anything; we could have understood from her gaze, from her gleaming eyes, when we were leaving and she said goodbye to us outside the front door in Piazza Cottolengo. It was the last time, out of the house. Turning, we saw her still: she was standing there, her face slightly lowered, as if to hold back or conceal something. No doubt she knew. Her ardent eyes seemed to follow us.

Innocenzo said: 'I knew in April, that I had to go.' We were in Camogli, in April, and I titled my thoughts *Minima mortalia*. They were notes, aphorisms, and naturally it was a play on 'moralia': I meant 'thoughts on mortality'. Flashes that were almost immortal in their revealing themselves ephemerally. I continued writing them in Courmayeur and then I lost them.

It could have been an unconscious premonition, the choice of that word. He had felt back pain, and had a wooden board put under the mattress, or a hard mattress, I don't remember – like for a normal bout of pain. And instead he already knew? I didn't have the slightest suspicion.

We spent a lot of time looking at the sea, and in the evening the boats going out to fish, black and thin (Chinese images) against the gleaming sea. 'Boats are so beautiful because they're ancient and always the same,' Innocenzo said.

53

The Assyrian lions at the British Museum, wounded, dying, were the ultimate revelation. Two years in a row – before, they weren't there – we stopped for a long while in those underground rooms; and the second time we didn't know it was the last.

I wrote a note then: 'Tragic beauty of death in noble animals. Salvation in beauty – contemplation – meditation – engagement – catharsis.' Later – I can deduce as much from my writing – I added: 'Beauty as salvation. Consequence: to clean beauty of hedonism – and salvation of fanaticism.'

An image that could speak for them all: that of the mortally wounded lioness, with an arrow stuck high in her back, dragging herself on her front paws, her head raised in a roar-scream of pain.

54

Life – ours – had reached a summit. The last loving breakfast at Piperno, in the small piazza. Between shade and light. Only the two of us, and a gentle wind blowing through the set and empty tables. Usually we went in the evening. For the first time I walked over to see, from up close, the old, dry fountain.

Tranquil happiness. Deluded – maybe I alone – by the bliss of that moment. His anaemia had been defeated by six transfusions. Delusion, I don't think so. Knowing abandon – and not regrettable. Gratitude, actually. Almost a guarantee (of deliverance? certainly not from suffering nor from the end) of a non-elusive – rather, conclusive – sense of the present.

In Rome, going back forever, I had always tried to be alone with him. There, I had never felt truly loved.

55

I don't know if they were what could be called symptoms, as they say or as they used to say in medicine. These signs were hardly any at all. The first, very vague, not alarming in the slightest, and in a certain way pitiful: it couldn't not be, insofar as it was a crack in his physical perfection. For a while I'd noticed, when going into the bathroom after him, something that wasn't what one might suppose, which lingers even after the water's been flushed and air has been let in. It wasn't a bad smell, only strange: a faint coating of his usual aroma. I pieced together that it was due to the use of suppositories (a remedy for constipation). I called it 'une odeur fade'.

The second warning came to me from an image. I didn't think of it as one of old age, but of tiredness. Not even: it was an infinitely sad image, but I didn't consider it prophetic; I registered it, but I never brought it up with him during the day.

I'd see him at times, from behind, sitting on the edge of the bed, bent over to adjust part of his nightclothes, and he seemed to me a rummaging beggar, hunched over his rags, seated on the kerb of the pavement.

It's a fleeting image in the span of a long life; and yet eternal: in the sense of 'for ever'. From which you can't go back.

56

First it was his pallor, at a dinner: I saw from afar, thought I was the only one who saw; but the next day Bruna called me, alarmed: 'Innocenzo was very pale last night.' So it was true. I called Clerici. In his bloodwork there consistently appeared the sharpened signs of 'myeloma', a term more mysterious than menacing. It would be possible to exorcize it, since it wasn't *progressing*; and the horror it pointed to was pushed back to late old age: this was the sentence they gave him. Like for children, far-away horror isn't scary. Even the medical professor, an eminent haematologist who'd first spotted the malevolent signs during an operation, simply suggested a stay in the mountains.

My idea now – then it was a suspicion – is that Clerici, a general doctor, attentive but on the outside laid-back, knew. With the continuation of the story, I can only praise, admire his prudence, his wisdom, his charity.

57

Not in one of our adventurous cabins any more but, by necessity, in a Grand Hotel. The double room had a window facing the Grandes Jorasses, and of the town could be seen only the small and pathetic Romanesque bell tower. That hotel room became one of my 'homes', like room no. 4 in the Carrel Pension in Cheneil, like the room with a view of the plane trees in Hyde Park in London.

He didn't sleep at night. I saw that every now and then he'd feel his pulse. 'Why are you feeling your pulse? Try to sleep instead.' Idiotic and cruel suggestion. Then I'd fall back asleep. Again I see him, standing in front of the window, looking at the small illuminated bell tower.

Things were easier during the day. In the meadow, in the sun – but he didn't tan as he once did – he read. Every now and then I went out: to walk.

In the evening after lunch we sat in the large hall-bar, which was long like a cathedral, with many wide and deep sofas; low to the ground ran enamel decorations – mountain animals and skies – while on the walls hung a big painting, dark and veristic, of old Courmayeur, and many antique prints of the valley and mountain. From his corner, a professional, accompanying himself on the piano, sang sentimental arias into a microphone, with a southern sweetness, but playfully too. A few couples danced. The singer asked for requests. I – 'unfortunate soul' – responded. I threw out old ditties, for example 'Violino tzigano', 'Un'ora sola ti vorrei'. I had suggested to Innocenzo that he bring down a book; he didn't say anything, and so I thought that it wasn't a good suggestion. With this I somewhat explain to myself my incredible participation. Or maybe the 'frivolity of fear' was already at work in me.

58

That morning, on the large rocks down in the Val Veny, in the cold wind, he was, with his English cap and his hand on his walking stick, an 'old gentleman'; in fact, to me he already seemed a little bit someone else. But Mimmina Foà spoke to him so lovingly that he smiled, as if he still felt like himself – while so unlike himself with that demeanour in the mountains. (She too had already received her sentence, and she knew it.)

I looked in the direction of the glacier, almost black in that leaden light. On top of a natural terrace or overhang, like on the crest of a motionless wave, an array of people stood – maybe they couldn't climb up further? nor go down, even? – lined up as though for an execution. They seemed terrified to me, but also resigned.

59

There was that line of poetry which was so beautiful, about summer, 'season of dense climates…'

Shakespeare has the speaker say to his lover: 'Shall I compare thee to a summer's day?'

Once, for our anniversary, Innocenzo thought back on that sonnet (I believe). He never forgot the date; I, a few times. 'Why did you send me flowers?' I'd ask. For our twentieth, he wrote on a note that accompanied the flowers: 'Twenty years: a single summer's day.' He had absorbed that image, and recreated it.

For me, the summer is frightening, and its approach distressing. I always felt it as separation, distance. The excess of light, too, oppresses me; like midday, which for me is black. In a dream, I had happened to think of this image of summer: 'the funerary fringes' (of horses dressed in mourning?).

And yet as a period of time I now feel that August – the last – as stretched out, boundless and, in a certain way, even happy.

60

In the city the summer is more summer, and the light blacker. Leaving a restaurant I noticed his pallor, just barely veiled by the golden-brown colouring from the mountain sun. At our front door, Innocenzo suddenly looked like a ghost to me. He said: 'I'm exhausted' – but only as if to suggest it, almost apologizing.

The medical professor – like all professors – had left the city. Clerici said: 'My wife's no longer with us; I don't care about going on summer holiday.' He made arrangements for blood transfusions and came to our home every day, even twice a day.

I had for my own part a handicap. An idiot driver (a Milanese engineer), while backing up without looking, ran me over; I broke my fall with my right hand, and the next day a bone doctor confirmed that my wrist was broken and he made me a cast. My left hand was the only means I had at my disposal. Rachele ('everyone has their cross to bear,' she said) was in Belluno, and the building concierge left too. But I didn't have any real trouble. I took care of food at a fabulous delicatessen, with the cheerful name of Rossi & Grassi. I don't know how to use the washing machine, but I was able to change the sheets, towels and all that for the transfusions by digging into the linen closet. During the nights my arm felt heavy. Truly nothing is only negative: that added limitation better inserted me into the context of the situation, counterbalanced my excessive good health.

'You're very well!' the doctor who came for the transfusions said while leaving, and he'd look at me, almost scrutinize me, with surprise and even admiration.

Mr Tagliaferri would fleetingly appear: he brought papers from the bank, mail; most of the time he left it downstairs in the lobby. 'I think,' Innocenzo said, 'Tagliaferri didn't take his holiday this year.'

61

Naturally I was well: like in war, there's no getting sick. But why do I now think of that August as a time to be mourned? I didn't *know*. This doctor, who was from the blood-donation association, reassured me about his myeloma: a very long time, et cetera.

Every day Clerici declared to me, as though sharing glad tidings: 'His pressure is good!'

He palpated him too, and mentioned, but only in passing: 'There's a little toughness here…'

I am sure that he had understood; and I am also sure that he found informing me pointless. He said instead: 'While there's life, one has to live as best one can.'

In the early afternoon, during the transfusions, with Clerici and the other doctor, Innocenzo would talk. I'd isolate myself in the half-light of the little sitting room, in the light blue armchair which then became his, and, without wanting to, I'd fall asleep; I'd wake up when the blood doctor was leaving, to say goodbye.

I spoke with this doctor, later, of those conversations. He told me that Innocenzo recounted his journeys. 'And while I thought he talked about the bank…'

I was devastated. The regret, the remorse, was a new pain: as if that loss – having forgone listening – were the keenest, the most irreparable.

62

One day that month, I wrote on a little sheet of paper: 'I have no hope, but still confidence. Faith?' There's the date too: 16-8-'84. Later I added on the same sheet: 'Faith means confidence, therefore hope. But if there's hope, it must come from resignation.' Maybe this was even a stroke of wisdom, if it meant: We'll be given our due. Or: I'll have the strength. Or: He won't have to suffer too much. Maybe it was rather *peace*. The peace of necessity.

Towards the end of the month Clerici freed me from my cast. I went to see the professor, who had returned to the city and came over right away. He too understood, I believe; he said that he'd have Innocenzo admitted that very evening to the clinic, which had just reopened.

63

He stayed only three days in the clinic. The third day he had a CAT scan. When they brought him back to the room, I went out into the hallway. The professor: 'Don't say anything to your husband.' I asked only: 'The myeloma?' 'No, it doesn't have to do with his myeloma.' I didn't ask anything else. In the room I said nothing to Innocenzo, but only because there was no need to. He said: 'I'd like to go home, and not come back here again.' 'You don't have to have surgery, so you'll stay home.'

The next day, a September morning; deep blue sky, the air crystal clear. I go out for the newspapers. On Corso di Porta Romano, I see the professor walking down towards me. A very handsome man, with transparent eyes. From some mysterious impulse, I kiss his hand: maybe I saw in him the Master (of life). I ask: 'How much time?' A few weeks.

Everything went dark. That was it, the true sentence. In that moment I lost him, I knew I had lost him.

Suddenly time had been cut frighteningly short; like for a person plummeting who sees moving towards her the ground where she'll be crushed.

64

In that clinic, Bacchelli had been staying as a patient for years. By now blind and deaf, he was still his old self in rare moments of lucidity; grander, in fact, honed in spirit. I had gone to see him; his nurse recognized me and pointed me to his room. I knocked, and as soon as I entered I saw him, I don't know whether sunk down or propped upright: an enormous, white monument. Imposingness suited him. But he started squealing, like an abandoned, hungry infant. The nurse was eating a fruit in the corner. I took in the extent of that humiliation.

Before leaving the clinic, Innocenzo wanted to say goodbye to him; the nurse shouted into his ear who we were, and he said: 'Friends, good friends.' Innocenzo, disoriented by the weakness of his tall body, looked at him with deep respect and pity. He was the one who needed to die first. Each, again, gets his due.

65

If we could choose between the violence of a sudden death and the patience of a long stretch of time, perhaps we'd choose the latter. But 'a few weeks' was like a bolt of lightning. I decided to slow time down. It became *largo, lento, pianissimo*; even though, as in a classical sonata, it then had to end with a rapid tempo: an *allegro tragico*.

I wrote then (September '84): 'We count time no longer in years, but by months, then by weeks, by days. Except that these months, days, hours, are centuries.'

Centuries for the gravity of the metamorphosis that took place. A cosmic slowness distended time, because the time was so little.

66

I wasn't sure if Clerici knew the name of the affected organ; they certainly must have spoken about it, he and the professor. He didn't bring up the topic with me, nor did I with him in order to find out. Innocenzo knew too, no doubt without knowing the name, like me. (It was an elegant name, Greek; I found out much later, without enquiring: one of those organs that you hear named only at school when studying the human body.) For him it was enough to know that he 'had to go away'. He made a quick gesture, suggesting a goodbye, departure.

He had always loved departures. In airports, upon arrival, he'd turn to look at the planes ready to leave, and say: 'I'd like to board another one!'

Back then, a departure meant a beginning. More than departing, now it seemed to mean distancing, 'moving off'. To be dead is to be absent. To die is to set out towards absence.

67

An 'expressionist' poem, I believe from the Forties, has very powerful imagery, sparked by the anguish of separation:

> you go far off
> and after you I unleash the pack
> of panting bloodhounds
> the imploring army
> will reach you wherever
> listen: in the sky above
> senseless angels
> desperately cry your name.

This last image is figurative (medieval): the angels are from Giotto's *Deposition* in Assisi. Only now does that power gain meaning: it was a presentiment, prescience. But in that hopeless September there was instead restraint, silence.

I had found out from Maria that when I was ill in the Sixties and a doctor had told Innocenzo that I might have cancer, he used to go in the kitchen to cry. For me there were no tears, not even in secret. I knew with certainty, and mine was 'despair's composure'.

68

The transfusions were interrupted, and there came medicines, pills, drops, which were supposed to get rid of the blood in his stool. Minimal, meticulous things; not repugnant. However, they sharpened his fits of pain, the ones that had started for the first time one night in June and which I hadn't understood – pain he'd recorded in his pocket journal as 'excruciating'.

Clerici prescribed certain suppositories, which I handed to Innocenzo in the evening; they were preceded by the pinkish pills of the analgesic Optalidon in the afternoon. Every day Clerici reassured me about his blood pressure (for me, flatus vocis). He made conversation light-heartedly, cheerfully. He talked about himself. He had been a brilliant cavalry officer in his youth; he chose a profession over a career; he'd originally had technical schooling. 'Isn't it funny?' he said. When his wife died, years earlier, we saw in the newspaper that she was a countess. 'So you're a count,' I said once. 'Yes, yes,' he admitted, shrugging his shoulders. His nose was undoubtedly aristocratic, and his round eyes behind his thick lenses gave him an inquisitive air. The professor had told us that he brought him as an example for his students at the start of every new class: 'If you want to see a real doctor in the flesh, go at eight in the morning to Via Donizetti and you'll see a slim, bald man walking briskly with a black bag under his arm. It's him, already off to see a patient.'

69

It was, as I said, a slow 'tempo', *largo*, waning. He himself made a sign with his hand of sinking with each day, slowly lowering the palm of his hand. I didn't contradict him. It was as if he were verifying it and sharing, knowing the seriousness without diminishing or accentuating it. I made no comment; I didn't want to deceive him, nor would I have wanted for him to deceive himself. I had too much respect for him and for death.

There was not, and we did not look for, consolation. There was the assistance of Clerici, of Tagliaferri. The loyalty of humility.

The days went in the following manner: Clerici would arrive early, then he'd get up, go to the bathroom and shave; after that, leaning on me he'd take a seat, always in the same armchair next to the window. I'd sit on the little bench in front of him, look at him. To myself, I called death *the Man-Flayer*.

70

Grand old men appear throughout painting; the prophets of the mosaics, with their pool-like eyes, their solemn hieratic heads. But Rembrandt's old men and 'himself as an old man' have always spoken to me and I couldn't even fully understand why. All of them, but especially the one who posed for his Aristotle in the Metropolitan, caressing the head of Homer – all of them were my intimate companions in life. Painting and person are one, in these cases; above all the old man with the velvet cap in the National Gallery; I'd stop a long while in front of him, each year. I so loved that profoundly aware, profoundly sad – not desperate – infinitely tired gaze. Innocenzo was that old man, the last month. How he appeared meditative and at the same time absent, surrendered. In front of Rembrandt's old men, those sad eyes staring into the void, I would wonder: Do they think? No. They know.

71

'The disciples sleep while Jesus is on the Mount of Olives, and he later chastises them. And I sleep while he suffers.' I thought this thousands of times when he paced up and down with a migraine, holding his head in his hands, and I slept; I didn't want to, but I'd plunge back into sleep without realizing.

And so things went at the clinic, too, when after an operation he had two very serious infections; then, however, I was ready to wake up as soon as he made the slightest noise to call for me; he ran very high fevers, I'd give him something to drink, then I'd drop off again, starved of sleep: with rage, but powerless.

In September, on the other hand, I defeated my drowsiness. I did not sleep; it was, I think, my will not to abandon him for even a second. While he was under the effects of the analgesic, I read.

Since I never rebel against chance, which I consider a necessary occasion – that is, fate – I slipped between the stacks of books on and underneath my bedside table another little book. It had a 'clinical' origin, since it was a gift I'd received from an old, retired colleague of Innocenzo's, who reached out only whenever he was hospitalized, naturally out of shyness. A compilation of the four Gospels, a paperback Catholic edition.

72

And so I read the Gospels. I had read them many times, but this time I read them as a novel. A reading that was an end in itself. I was struck by their naturalness; the kind one finds only in imaginary stories full of truth. It was not the sacred, not even salvation. It was truth as clear as air and as hearty as bread. It was therefore direct in meaning; deep down I had always known this, but I suspected that it was just a convenient impression. It didn't seem convenient, but simple. As Piero said as a boy, God shouldn't speak through enigmas (like the gods). What every so often emerged, and was inherent to the 'culture' of the time (the damning, the invectives), never seemed essential to me: such things were actually extraneous, clashed. It seemed clear to me that Jesus wanted to free people precisely from the sacred, from ritual, from tradition. It was reassuring.

But remotely for me – stranded there at a last resort.

73

From inattention to dedication, perhaps. I won't say to self-abnegation, which would be too much, as a word and as a thing. My dedication came naturally. It was all there was left for me. If it's true that one has what one can give. But I was still myself, after all. And there came a moment, which now seems monstrous to me: a moment of impatience. Not an outburst, but a suggestion made in complete thoughtlessness.

In my nature as a non-housewife companion, there had never been a place for any knowledge of, let alone care for, male apparel. (Andreina had surprised me when she said as a little girl: 'I know how men's jackets are made.') In this I had stayed a spinster. Now I helped him get dressed, and I had no patience for it. It was so complicated: pull up the socks, tuck in the undershirt, the shirt… I said: 'Couldn't you use your robe?'

I didn't understand that it meant: You'll never be dressed again. And he accepted it, because he was still the one understanding and indulging me.

74

For fear of getting things dirty – though it never happened – he wanted to get up and go to the bathroom many times during the night. Lying awake, I would run, circling around my side of the bed, and would reach him in time. Having already set his legs down, he'd straighten up while leaning on me, rest an arm on my shoulders. I accompanied him, with small steps. It was gentle, that arm – as it had always been. But once, despite running I didn't make it in time: he slid down to the floor. For the first and only time I wept, I sobbed from powerlessness, as I tried to pull him up. He had lost a lot of weight, but he was still too heavy for me. He managed on his own, resting his elbows on the edge of the bed. After this I resigned myself to calling on the nurses, as had been suggested to me for some time.

75

The two nurses. The day nurse was a handsome young man, sunny as his role implied: efficient, indifferent. As I had feared, he sat down close to him; I didn't see the need for this and tried to tone down his presence: I told him to have a seat not so close. He took the farthest armchair. There were economic studies around, brought over by Tagliaferri: the young man began to flip through them and actually read them, apparently with interest. Innocenzo smiled. This nurse helped him with his morning routine of shaving and getting dressed, and he was great at it, Innocenzo said. And so I was grateful to him.

The one at night was duly nocturnal: reserved, taciturn, thoughtful. He read in his armchair by the secondary entrance, from where he could hear and see into the bedroom; he would rush in, quick and silent. Only in the morning would he accept a slice of breakfast cake. He was enrolled in medicine and worked as a nurse to pay his tuition fees; in fact, he didn't read, he studied. I really loved him, I never forgot him.

76

I even felt a sort of gratitude for the suppositories that lulled him to sleep. It had happened with my mother too; when there's no cure, I at least want suffering to be eased. I have no trouble admitting that this is part of my own selfishness: I can't bear for a person to suffer pointlessly. And I am not just impatient; I fear physical pain like something alien, a violence that impedes a person from being themself. I know that sedatives dull the senses too, can cause one's memory to fade, and life without memory is already death. Mamma, once so lucid, would ask: 'Is Papà still with us?' (dead for years); or: 'And Pierino?' She didn't remember, whereas not even a month earlier she had been so happy to see him there, sitting at the foot of her bed.

Innocenzo, who had an acute sense of how much in this world is comedy – not just mediocrity, but hypocrisy, vanity, trickery – hadn't lost that sense: he found it once again in the deception of the medicines and the analgesics. He called them a charade: like those of politicians. With the nurse, before an injection, more than once he said clearly: 'Another charade.'

77

One night, in the drowsy state induced by the analgesic, Innocenzo spoke. I was bent over him and I heard him say distinctly: 'The first to teach us to die was Tolstoy.'

We had never named death; and yet he had it so present within him that his first 'free' thought was this. It was horrible, for me; but it was a kind of comfort that he had thought of Tolstoy, and as a teacher: a religious teacher, not in the preachy sense of recent years, but in the vital, total sense of his realism. I then reflected that he must have been thinking of *The Death of Ivan Ilyich*. We had read it in Cuneo, it had been recommended to us by our friend Turin. That frightening death, his loneliness in that egotistical bourgeois family, his final acceptance. But Innocenzo loved all of Tolstoy, especially *Anna Karenina*; and several times we had reread *War and Peace* together.

78

He wasn't talking to me, wasn't looking at me.

'Look at me, I'm here.'

'I'm the one who's not here.'

It was awareness – therefore the presence – of his *diminutio* (so I called to myself his nearing the end). It was like a growing of non-presence. A dwindling of his being there. ('*Being there* is all we have,' I wrote once.) I perceived an elusiveness, and at the same time a majesty born of the elusive. Almost an affirmation: of 'no-longer-being'. The affirming, ultimately, of an extreme powerlessness.

79

He's absorbed, sad. 'What are you thinking about?'
'About reality.'

I was prepared to face the truth. But now I think: was it a victory of the material? Hofmannsthal says that 'every man takes a secret with him when he dies: how it was possible for him – spiritually – to live'. What Clerici called 'biological fate', too, can be lived spiritually. Innocenzo no doubt meant his very real condition: his diminished, waning vitality. A frightening and fatal reality, about which he didn't want to delude himself. If I hadn't asked, he wouldn't have said anything. It was an acceptance. Not proclaimed, not even asserted. Merely said.

Materialism, too, can be great. Sad, but from contemplation. Severe awareness, firmness that isn't flaunted; or actually: indifference (in his sense of the term), irony. What he meant was also: there's no place for joking around (hence the charade medicines).

80

Was his silence meditation too? I can't rule this out; it seems impossible that the intensity of his rare laconic words was not the peak of long and drawn-out thought. Into his last – interrupted – journal were slipped many little pages where he had transcribed lines of poetry (Dickinson, Shakespeare, Borges), thoughts. One, by Canetti: '…but only the thoughts no one knows anything about keep a man alive'. Behind his silence there was this vertigo (for me).

He had no need for consolation; but something tempted me. I didn't dare, it seemed hypocritical to propose a prayer. Hypocritical, sentimental: things he hadn't been in love, should we have been them in death? And besides, a prayer does not need to be *said*. He had always really liked what you hear in church at funerals: 'Our brother who has fallen asleep in the *hope* of the resurrection.' I wanted to know his thoughts on this. I said: 'Men, civilizations, religions have always thought that we'll see each other again…' Would I have been happy if he said, 'I hope so'? But it wasn't possible. What he said is the key to all of him. He said: 'I make no demands.'

81

I don't think just anyone can understand. Maurizio Mattioli understood when I told him, I believe immediately 'after'; he had already understood why Innocenzo always sat at the back. Extreme humility: but in the sense of utter disinterest, not a desire to be humble. It can come across as pride; it's nonchalance, discretion. It's also a Piedmontese trait: 'Give me whatever I deserve,' Pavese would say when someone was hosting a gathering. It seemed only his sense of humour, but there was a philosophy underneath. Was it – Innocenzo's – stoicism? How he had liked Storoni's words about Marcus Aurelius! But more than that he had a Christian humility. Certainly not devotional: secret.

'I make no demands' brings to light how much vanity there is in every prospect of reward, of recognition. Once again, his *indifference*.

82

I am neither stoic nor devout. I considered my state of hopelessness – in the sense of non-hope – a good foundation for serenity. For him it was definitely so. But at a certain point I found myself standing before an abyss. I needed help. I prayed countless times in life, including in the literal sense of saying Hail Marys; but now I could not. I remembered Augustine: 'Go down into yourself.' It was an instant: it saved me.

It was so true, that I later resisted the temptation to repeat what I'd experienced in that instant. It could destroy it, reduce it to an expedient.

83

I said: 'I'll hate everyone, after.' That's exactly what I said: 'after'. It was always implied, that *after*; it could be named, because it was part of reality. He said: 'No, we aren't capable of hating.' I felt gratitude for that 'we'. I meant I'd hate everyone because they were alive (myself included); he caught the excessive, wretched term.

'How should I be? Good?'

And he, with a smile: 'As always…'

The smile meant: 'You couldn't be any different from how you are.' It seemed a certainty, an infinitely indulgent one. Would God's judgement be harsher? I too must learn to 'make no demands'.

He showed indulgence, with me, gentleness; not a need for me. Nothing was now denied, but not re-evoked either. He was already *beyond*. I don't mean in the eternal: only 'no-longer-here'.

84

Why do I say 'need'? The need for security that can come only from being sure that you are loved. Some people long for childhood and parents even in old age. I never found out, nor did I ever ask, if it was so – or how it was – for him.

When I was the one who was ill, with an illness I couldn't name, I'd catch – at the table, he opposite me – his intense, penetrating gaze, staring straight into my eyes. It was a frightening interrogation. It was also a form of strength, his limitless stamina in granting support.

Some doctors (who must not have been the sharpest around) had examined me, treated me; but I stayed unwell all the same, without suffering physically (while I'd always feared physical pain: I can't bear it). I lived in a state devoid of any love for life. He understood and looked at me that way. I let him take me to the Polyclinic where a good doctor recognized my malady. I got better rapidly. It was then that Maria told me that he'd go into the kitchen to cry. He, crying… I hadn't suspected it; I didn't say a word about it to him. I thought back on it when he was dying, and I told myself: So I haven't been wrong to hide my fear from him, my despair. I was right not to abandon myself to it. Also in the sense that 'I acted like him'.

85

Occasionally a light joy would rise up from deep inside him – maybe it's true, as Savinio said, that depth is on the surface – tranquil, without any yearning for the past. Maybe it drew on the eternal present which never sets, as long as some fragment of memory is left.

'We had beautiful moments,' he said. 'Emiliano in our arms at night…'

Here too he involved me, those moments were ours; and here too I was grateful for his being aware of my presence.

He also played games of the imagination, and had fun doing so, albeit feebly. Visual analogies that he had always made, but more sudden. There were roses, on the low table in the living room; he looked at them and said: 'Do you see that rose sticking out? It's the head of an Irish priest, with red hair' (the rose was an orange-pink colour).

One joke verged on horror, and was thereby, in its lightness, tragic. Clerici, who every so often took up his 'biological fate' theme again, said, 'All of us have our Achilles' heel.' Clerici never spoke sententiously, if not to be funny, and sure enough he added: 'I didn't have a classical education, but I know what the expression means.' That evening Innocenzo smiled almost mischievously, right before swallowing two Optalidon pills. 'Why are you smiling?' 'Because Optalidon can't do anything against Achilles' heel.'

86

To bring him to his armchair after helping him get dressed, the day nurse pushed him on a metal wheelchair. He sat erect, rigid, as if this ceremony called for it. I thought of my father, who'd always made an effort to give dignity to his demeanour in old age, with his diminished strength; he too tried to straighten up, keep his head high.

One morning, in the middle of that act which must very well have been voluntary, Innocenzo seemed absent. Reaching me by the front entrance, the nurse said: 'Here's your better half!'

I hated him; then I remembered that servant-nurse in the hospital in Alessandria when Grandpa Edoardo (the General) was dying: 'How old are you?' she asked him, and other irreverent idiocies.

The nurse called me from the bathroom door, waving me over as though for something amusing. He is moving the electric razor around his face, keeping it at a distance, and looking at himself in the mirror, as if he is actually shaving. The nurse laughs. I feel cold, an arctic cold; but the feeling is also rapture. The scene has a mysterious beauty, an enigmatic solemnity. It is still his innate hieratic grace, once again, now grand in its absurdity.

> We did not know
> that the eternal is a tempest
> now we tremble
> in our miserable vestments
> in the arctic wind

87

Innocenzo always had for religion more or less the same absence of passion that he had for philosophy: as opposed to me. But while he was never interested in philosophical 'problems', he was in truth philosophical, at least in the sense of 'wise'. Similarly, he was more religious than I was, but in a different way, by which I mean without any interest in theology. For a certain period of time he felt tempted by the Protestant Church, but then he discovered that they too were holier-than-thou.

It had never cost him a great effort to be observant, then without any drama he stopped practising. However, he expressed – and more than once – this fundamental judgement: 'Without religion means without poetry.'

In those days towards the end, I didn't even ask myself the question, and not because it was antiquated: whether to call the priest. I did however consult Liliana, the only person who knew him well, in a certain sense better than I did (insofar as she wasn't so personally involved), and she, Catholic and I believe devout, said: 'He could give the sermon to the priest.'

In the Fifties at the Aurora, one of the cinemas on Via Paolo Sarpi, I'd seen a film that I never came across again. It had Spencer Tracy, with his kind and clever face, who had created a scandal over religious observance (in America, naturally), and to the judge who asked him 'What religion are you?' he replied: 'None.' 'Why?' 'For my religion.'

This declaration and Innocenzo's on religion as a poetic outlook can be placed side by side.

88

Innocenzo had had a religious teacher: a Capuchin, in Perugia, when he was in middle school. He'd cross the town, towards the Monterotondo monastery; in the working-class neighbourhoods the rascals in the street made fun of him, shouted after him because he wore short, white trousers, which were also too wide: like his winter coats, they were his uncle the naval officer's. He bore it, because Father Anselmo was his great friend.

His mother, who forcefully maintained order in the family, subjected her children to strict discipline for the health of the body and the soul. A purgative every fifteen days, and once a month confession and communion. Father Anselmo was the one to take his confession; he'd say to him, 'Sit here,' and, seated close together on the bench, they'd chat.

He spoke to me often of Father Anselmo, and I always insisted that he go to see him. But he feared he wouldn't find him again; and maybe, like for the young girls he'd loved, he feared the meeting itself. In Perugia, on holiday, he made up his mind and we went to look for him. We walked up steep steps between cypresses, then I, barred from the enclosed order, waited for him seated on a low wall. Father Anselmo was the same as ever; he said to him: 'I hope you've stayed good. But not too uptight!'

Father Anselmo had a double, by way of contrast. He was big, bearded, his tunic shabby; Father Tito was young, virile, elegant. 'Those friars from Assisi,' Father Anselmo said, 'eat meat as often as once a week!' He meant that through contact with pilgrims, tourists, they had been a bit corrupted. Father Tito was Innocenzo's mother and little sisters' confessor. He'd composed a prayer for his mother. It started and ended with 'hear me!' Father Tito had given (or maybe only shown) her a photo of himself in military uniform.

89

Piero would come, and run off; the nurses said that sons all do that (more fragile, compared to daughters, in the face of death). Marlène had come with the children, who were serious and calm; she entertained Innocenzo with financial questions (met with impatience on my part). I wasn't informing anyone; not only was I protecting our final solitude, but I also feared his generosity and therefore the fatigue of it all. Colleague friends (big shots) came, Liliana with her boss (she brought the roses, the Irish priest ones). Everyone was very discreet: affectionate but serene, detached. Perfect. Except that their perfection was loathsome (to me), for what it presumed.

On the eve of the last day – not of life, of word – three colleagues (mid-high tier) asked to see him the next day. I didn't want them to come, but I asked him. He had me give him a piece of paper and tried to write their names. Gradually, the messy letters were traced out, as though by an illiterate person. It wasn't the abstract, faux writing that Gramigna recreated in his *Impious Aeneas*, or the kind my aunts in Cuneo had said Grandpa Michele used to scribble onto his notebook: writing as painting – poignant, poetic, but impersonal. In him it was the attempt, the will to keep giving. Maybe only a residual will to be. He tried, though not stubbornly, and gave up. Nodding, he conveyed to me that he'd see them.

90

A bearded face like a boyish Marx – kind and knowing – Ettore came, on Saturday morning. With him the last conversation took place. There was a fatherly and at the same time fraternal bond between them.

I had the idea of boiling a seabass for him, which he liked: Ettore fed him, and he smiled back; he asked him about Urbino, about the professor, about his work.

In the evening: his colleagues, the ones whose names had been written with so much effort the day before. They came in turns. The first (I didn't know him), pudgy, awkward, sat in front of him on the low chair and unfolded a piece of paper for him to see, a letter. He looked at it, motionless, and in a certain sense attentive. Maybe he could see, he had smiled when this colleague arrived, but he couldn't read. 'What is it?' I asked. 'It's from the man who had him made Grand Cross!' Idiot, I thought. 'He didn't care about that at all,' I said, 'you can imagine if he does now.' I frightened him, he hurriedly said his goodbyes. The second was a real friend, with a sharp mind. He tried to act natural. 'How are you doing, Innocenzo, are you managing to sleep?' He didn't respond and his friend understood; he was a delicate person. The third, a handsome and tall, authoritative man, did not even take a seat. He said only, 'I'll come back Monday,' and he cast a pained look at me. The driver told me later that he had placed a hand on his shoulder (and he's not one to act overly familiar), saying, 'What is life…'

Devoted, embarrassed, these three bureaucrats: like tragic Magi.

91

That evening brought a joy. Was such a thing possible? Unforeseeable, yes, but it was presented naturally, even solemnly. Marlène appeared, as though bearing an offering. Serious as always, she was holding a parcel with two hands: light blue. Wrapped in a plastic bag, a plate covered by another, flipped-over plate, and inside it, two slices of a roast: big, good-smelling, still warm. She said: 'I thought, in moments like these, you could use it.'

Immediately I recalled the first time we visited them on Via Colletta (Maria was there too), and Piero saying, 'You couldn't get a roast?'

Nourishment this time, too, something providential. I sensed almost a promise. In those days I myself had said to Innocenzo: 'My new family will be Marlène and the children.'

But that gesture of offering was not a promise.

92

Sunday. Clerici appears, for the first time without a smile, his big eyes, doubled by his lenses, bulging: 'Signora, his pressure has gone down!'

I've never grasped the importance of good blood pressure; now I understand everything from those two alarmed eyes. What's more, I've always recognized his optimism as one of his ways of helping.

I am already still, I am not anxious. I am next to Innocenzo, Piero is there too. Giancarlo (our friar nephew) enters, arms raised, in his rich and wide outfit, which sways. He announces, beaming: 'Peace and goodwill. I've come from Assisi!'

His joy is real, but in this moment I reject it. He sits in front of him, very close. Innocenzo has a vague smile, he doesn't recognize him. The friar repeats: 'I've come from Assisi!'

I decide to intervene: I talk of Umbria, of Father Anselmo. Giancarlo presses on, still joyful: 'But I bring you news of Father Tito!' (he too knows the family stories, but seen from the opposite side). I say: 'Don't name Father Tito!'

Innocenzo doesn't hear; I identify with him (he who wouldn't have reacted with my violence). 'Why?' 'Your uncle couldn't stand him.' 'Really?'

Absence, which is already death, provokes the absurd, even comic side of things.

In the afternoon, on the intercom: his brother Nico and his wife. I go downstairs but I don't open. I talk through the gate; I have no hesitation. 'I'm not having anyone over,' I say, 'he's dying.' 'Maybe he'd like to see someone…' 'No, not him.' 'Then we'll go.' (They had come from Verona.) Nico is a serios man, handsome and proud: he looks not only heartbroken, but humble. I feel sorry for him.

93

Now the agony, the horror. No one has represented the torture of that final agony like Bacon. We'd gazed at it together for a long while, in London, many times. Especially that *Triptych*. The screaming, the fury, the disfigurement. And yet it is mercy. There is no mercy without mercilessness.

I stayed there, the whole night, the whole day after. I didn't want to not be there. For myself. When my mother died I'd already gone to sleep and Luciana came to wake me: 'Mammina is gone.'

His long and dry body was wrapped tightly in a blanket (the thin, dark-green plaid blanket). Rigid, tapered. Lofty and at the same time humble, humiliated. Surrendered. His intermittent breath – hoarse – a cry. Something alien. His arms kept tight in a linear constriction down to his elbows; his forearms bent, vertical, reaching; and the hands – *his* hands – curled, hooked, as though for a spasm of pain or a call for help. It wasn't like him. A gesture of powerlessness and almost of fury, of ultimate rage.

I thought, I managed to think that he was no longer there. The light in his eyes had gone out, under lowered lids. Doctor Legnani reassured me, after; they were electric discharges. That noise, too, was proof: had he been present, he would have felt ashamed to do anything so upsetting. I remembered *Cries and Whispers*, the hooked hand of the dying woman who couldn't die.

What's gruesome in death is therefore this: the agony of the animal. I was able to think it about him! But it was a good thought: he couldn't feel desperation.

The day nurse had gone into the other room; he couldn't take it, he said – and he a professional, a young man who had been numb to the majesty of the end over the previous days. It was too long, his death agony. I stayed; I did not want to miss a single minute of that residual presence, terrifying but also sweet, of some part of him.

94

Like when one pulls the plug, even more instantaneously the voice – it wasn't *his* voice – went silent.

I took the few steps from the bed to the telephone; but I was blocked by the day nurse. I wanted to call the bank (the mother), instead he immediately cautioned me: 'No, people will come right away,' (he knew what I was feeling) 'we'll take care of everything ourselves.'

I made the decisions for his clothing on my own, rapidly, but calmly and without second-guessing myself. I did not want the home to be invaded (I remembered other funerals), therefore he had to be laid out in the living room, which the entrance immediately faces. His suit, one dear to him: his blazer. A heavy decision was the funeral itself: I thought he would have approved of my choice. We had been active in a certain political direction, but we were free of ideology: an exclusive funeral wouldn't be called for. The traditional culture of our hometown and of our families was sufficient and not shameful; for years we had stayed on the margins 'for' our religion, like Spencer Tracy in that film, and not 'against' religion.

In terms of the nurse, he overstepped somewhat; I imagine for the usual reasons, which aren't completely dishonest ones in the end. Immediately a specialist arrived, looking appropriately funereal and abstract; he took command of the bedroom and I wasn't displeased to stay far away. Everything went hurtling down into the macabre-grotesque, until it verged on comical. Such was the tone and pace of that evening in which I became a widow – a term fit, again, for a comedy.

95

That sort of overstepping continued with the woman from the funeral home, a middle-aged fake blonde, not ugly but terrifying, extremely efficient. 'I've prepared a fabulous notice for you, they're my speciality, with an epigraph.' I hadn't planned it beforehand, but I'd written the death notice to show it to Piero. She looked at me with disdain, almost contempt, perhaps offended. She kept bringing up a strange word I didn't know: corser. I imagined that she was referring to an article of clothing – something between a corset and a collar – something that had to do with the manipulation of the body. 'Did you give some thought to the corser?'

But where her commercial-macabre parlance peaked was the coffin, which had to be made of fine wood. She showed various models, but insisted on suggesting one named 'Apollo'; in that coffin she had laid her deceased husband. Aesthetics were her forte: 'You'll thank me, when you see the flowers!'

By now Piero was there too: we avoided looking at each other, united by the same irresistible stimulus. We had laughed, with Innocenzo, in Paris, after seeing an ad for caskets: 'Pourquoi s'acharner à vivre... Why insist on living, when for a low price you can rest in a comfortable coffin?' Instead of that charming, light French cynicism, we were forced to laugh by the perverse, cruel humour of it all.

But Piero had brought me a message of freshness, one of life's small masterpieces. He'd arrived holding an envelope of sorts, between his palm and his thumb, like a child delivering a letter. Of sorts, because it was made of a sheet from a notebook folded in half and closed by folding again along its edges, as all of us did at some point as children, in the absence of an envelope. On the sheet was written: 'I have nothing to offer but inadequacy.' Thus, through Tullia, life itself let me know that it would give me endless consolation.

96

The next day he was a serene (filtered) image, even a bit wry (and how did the mysterious artificer do that, having never met him?). I regretted having looked. It was his form, but 'fake'. Like a successfully pulled-off imitation, in some non-perishable material. The last true image – peaceful, naturally – had been stolen from me, they had immediately sent me away. This 'new' image – I only looked at it for a moment, and I am already forgetting it (trying to).

The visitors came and admired him, someone caressed him, I believe Anna Russo (she had brought three white roses, and I put them next to him). I stood by his feet, greeting people.

Why of all people with Barbara and Maurizio – friends but not intimate ones – from what impulse did I remind them that two years earlier we'd had our golden wedding anniversary? And say, as I said, that that night was better than our wedding night, that it was much more beautiful? And add, still lightly, that the first night is always a bit embarrassing, isn't it? He smiled and agreed, if only out of politeness; she, Swiss and puritan, must have been scandalized.

I know: I couldn't stand for them to consider him 'deceased', or even for them to think of him as 'old'.

97

The parish priest at San Marco had asked Serafino: 'Who are these people who I never see in church?' Our building's (Tuscan) concierge replied: 'When you come to bless the house, have you ever found the door closed?' 'No.' 'And you've always found an envelope?' 'Yes.' 'There's your answer.'

The priest had heard about our friar nephew and had called him, and so the following day they celebrated together. When I still went to church I preferred the Carmine, purer, a Romanesque structure. San Marco was above all music. In a side chapel I had cried during Verdi's *Requiem Mass* (Silvia had died; but being moved by beauty is what inspires tears). That morning of the funeral I did not cry, I was turned to stone, I could not even see. Some things did stay imprinted in my memory: the embrace of Carlo Bombieri, who'd taken a plane from Rome, the wreath from the Levi-Montalcini sisters, who'd also come from Rome, Ester and her daughter looking like sisters, Lella Solmi paler than ever for a never-dormant pain of hers; all on her own, a girl was sobbing, tears streaming down her face: 'Who are you?' I asked her. She was Leda, Ugo's wife: 'For us, a father has died,' she said.

In the pew between Piero and Marlène, I realized that Piero was amused by his ex-wife's contrite demeanour, a mass-book in her hand: 'She doesn't know,' he whispered to me, 'that you can't be both concubine and devout.' I didn't respond, but I thought that the combination wasn't all that unusual. Meanwhile, to my surprise I found his friar cousin's homily good. The subject was Job's patience. Job's rebellion, the watered-down Catholic version, but expressed forcefully.

What I found out about from everyone later, and couldn't notice from my seat, was crying Emiliano, who'd run off from his grandmother Elsa and was desperately wandering up and down the naves. Bruna Cingano tried to console him; he hugged his friend Tagliaferri and asked him for a coin to light a prayer candle: 'For Grandpa.' *The Altar of the Dead*! Now for me the pity of James's story and Emiliano's pity are forever joined in the flickering flames of San Marco.

98

There was a family tomb (his family's) in Tortona; his brothers had had it turned into a marble palace. Innocenzo hadn't taken an interest, and his protests after everything had already been done only served to irritate his mother. He wasn't upset only for questions of taste, but because the names of their ancestors had disappeared, people of civil merit, as the tombstones dating back to the early nineteenth century had recalled. His protests ceased when his mother retorted: 'But they weren't even in the military!'

He made me a proposition: 'Writers should be buried where they were born. We can buy a plot of earth in the Demonte cemetery.' He drew a design for the simple grave: two stone slabs, a horizontal one with our names, a vertical one with a lightly engraved cross.

After the funeral in San Marco, a large number of us set out. Up there, Emiliano stayed by his father's side the whole time; the person who cried was Giulio Einaudi: he hadn't listened to Innocenzo in life, and now in a very human way he mourned him.

Giancarlo spoke too. He cited a psalm and alluded to biblical readings with his uncle (which never happened). I immediately acted rashly: I pointed out to him under my breath that his uncle didn't love the Bible, its moralizing. 'But I softened the text!' he said candidly. (It had also bothered me that he made Innocenzo sound like a zealot.) At his father's funeral, a few years before, Giancarlo had read Francis's *Canticle*. 'Our sister bodily Death'! It's the sole possible acceptance. In that *sister* everything is said. It's the recognition of fraternity, of a shared filial nature: death, too, redeemed as a creature. (Maybe this is the path to embracing the idea of divine creation, which is so difficult for me…)

99

In the car back to Milan, Piero asked me: 'Are you going to someone's tonight?' 'No, I'll go home.' 'If you want, you can eat with me.'

Talking with the character from *Light Words Between Us* was, as always, unpredictable. Solace flooded through me. I suggested he tell Tullia too. In the city – still in a fairy-tale atmosphere – Piero ran to a phone booth, and came back saying, 'Tullia says it would be more intimate at our place.' It's true that he was quoting her, but it was incredible all the same: 'intimate'!

And so I saw their studio for the first time, cluttered with beautiful useless things (antique or old), rare the useful things. I didn't recognize Tullia, whom I'd met only in London, for our golden wedding anniversary, when Piero, pretending (?) to arrive by coincidence, came to see us. I remembered a blonde girl with billowing hair; this one was brown-haired, with a straight bob, Louise Brooks style. Her eyes were the same: beautiful. Lots of little plates were scattered on the table for dinner, small bowls with various foods; without any advance notice she'd made the best out of what she had. Piero said: 'What a Renaissance feast!' When he teases, it's a sign that he's happy. And I was drunk from tiredness and joy.

100

Doctor Clerici had come, for the funeral, but I hadn't seen him. Rachele had seen him: he'd taken the service elevator. He was carrying a big bouquet of dahlias from a garden, not a florist. He said to Rachele, seeing her torn up: 'You see, the worst thing isn't death, it's solitude.' I hold on to all the words I heard come from him. I had never asked him for the name or the 'location' of the illness, I counted on talking to him about it *after*, on having him tell me many things about Innocenzo.

The first weekend was cruel, for me, not so much for his absence, even if it was in the background and had determined the circumstances; it was something else that happened. Monday Liliana called, speaking in her gently firm manner: 'Signora, there's bad news.' 'Can there still be bad news, for me?' I asked wearily. She had to tell me anyway. Clerici had died: suddenly, during the night. It was a new pain – no, a doubling of my pain – and integral, intrinsic to our story.

It was a continuation, and also a conclusion, as in a novel. I remembered the 'biological fate' which for him had thus been fulfilled – and mercifully, for that matter – along with his fate in the broader sense. For me it illuminated the meaning of death, which I was so passionate about and am still passionate about. I had this thought: in art, it is essential to stop in time; in life, death does it for us.

101

Maybe I was open to signs. I had an old shabby shelf, which I called 'the hospital' (in exhibitions, that's what they called the room for the not-rejected-out-of-pity paintings). From high up – without any apparent cause – a book fell.

Doctor Clerici had said how after the death of a famous theatre critic and friend, this very thing had happened: a book had fallen, inexplicably, from a shelf in the library where the body lay. The doctor, as positivistic as he was, was very shaken by the occurrence.

In my case, it was a book that I did not remember owning. A French book, from a random publisher, its title an indication of banality. I must have bought it in Paris. I flipped through the pages; it contained photographs interspersed with the text. Curled-up mummies, knees drawn in, their faces concealed. But I already possessed one of those images, which had been cut out from a magazine and had been hanging in my study for years as one of my points of reference (of meditation). Its emotional intensity is almost unbearable, but it's supported by a rigorous style (expressionist, baroque?), as in the most controlled work of art; whereas it is brutally, 'historically' real. Of the face, enclosed in cupped hands, one only sees a cheekbone and an eye socket from which a pained gaze seems to fall. It's despair – and even shame – but composure too. Like an unending, inconsolable cry. The book's images were instead twisted, mad with pain. Were they an allusion to 'his' agony? Of course, like that agony, they still belonged to life, to that remnant of life and to its indecipherable message.

102

A dream, too, is a sign. It comes from us, it is not an occurrence, and it is even more overwhelming (insofar as we're pulled into it).

'Why do they say that you're not here – you're here with me,' I was saying to him in the dream; and he was in front of me, seated, in his green corduroy suit, like in the photo in Campale. I hug him, and I wake up. It was excruciating. It had been a continuation, but illusory. I called Anna Russo and it came to me to synthesize it in this way: 'Presence is what brings out absence.'

Soon Giovanni came to see me. I don't know how he found out (he doesn't read newspapers). We see each other rarely, he always comes from far away. 'Giovanni, I feel that he's there, but where?'

We are still standing, his tall figure now slightly hunched, his clear eyes (navy blue) so penetrating, and yet distant.

'Giovanni, where are the dead?'

He responds gravely: 'Inside us.'

103

When Papà, after a fall on his bicycle, lost a lot of blood and we feared he might die, Mamma exclaimed in her rapid, immediate way: 'Our beautiful life is over!' That was her genius, defining her life with Papà as *beautiful*. She, so much better than I, so much kinder, more generous, more beautiful. In that 'our' is indeed the key.

Suddenly, in those days, to myself I called my life with Innocenzo 'a beautiful dream'. Perhaps I had woken up? I found the world beautiful as always, but tasteless. I saw too much, like that little girl of Ortese's after she put on glasses.

I also said to myself: 'a short dream'. Maybe because I'd had a relationship with a pure, perfect being. I recalled *Teorema*.

But why short? Happy hours can be long too. The bright June days that I called 'endless'. I said of the light in June

> …that has no end
> and through the clear night pierces

On those journeys in the car with Innocenzo, I'd sing to myself 'what a day – what luck…' (a song by Zanicchi, I think). Or that other one: '…la folie en tête…'

There was melancholy in that joy, as is only right; and it wasn't folly, but wisdom.

104

Saglio, in that discreetly fraternal way of his: 'You have to consider it an accident, a sudden death.' A real accident would have been even faster, and therefore more offensive. But it's true that the time of Innocenzo's decline was short. Only for a little while did I see him as old, and he didn't see me as old.

Childhood, adolescence: vast, infinite, but also in a certain sense lost. So, the one with him was not a dream, but my real life. And the ones I call other lives, in what has been the realest in them, are his too; not outside, but in his shadow (aura). Life with Papà and Mammina, Silvia, Luciana; and now with Piero, Emiliano and, as always, Giovanni. What is not *of him* is not good. It will be how I measure my life as it continues. So it must be.

I know that at the root of my love for him, as for Emiliano, there is the recognition of a substantive, irreducible *purity*. What Anna Esposito would say to me about Emiliano when he was a baby: 'Don't be afraid. No one can ruin him.' And now, through Emiliano, I come to understand Innocenzo better too. When he didn't share, didn't look for commiseration, which in our youth I attributed only to his consideration of me, he was also keeping silent in order not to cast any blame for not understanding him. Like Emiliano, who doesn't respond to my (overly passionate) requests to 'know'.

105

Of course, absolute purity is not human; love is. Purity is a nucleus, an indestructible kernel which is perhaps abstract, insofar as it's spiritual; whereas love is always concrete (as Hegel says of truth). In the hardest moments, of discouragement, I feel an urge to call out mentally: 'Mamma!' – and I realize that now my mother is him.

He had said that when he was young he hoped he'd die before me; then he had understood that it was better not to leave me alone. Luciana reminded me of that time in the Villar cemetery, where a tombstone showed that a couple had died just a few days apart, and his comment: 'Lucky!'

His brother Luigi: 'When we visited him, in August, he talked to us only about how your arm was in a cast, like it was his sole concern.' He was dying, and he knew it.

He had underlined these words of 'his' Shakespeare (from *Othello*): 'I loved without malice, but without measure.'

106

My mother was not laid waste like Innocenzo; she was in some way present for her own almost-absence. Perhaps due to less awareness? As always there was something fresh in her, almost infantile: 'There's that little gate…' she said. Our family tomb in Cuneo – a wall of burial cells – is in fact closed by an iron gate. It signified an obstacle, the difficulty of 'passing'. Even my legendary priest great-uncle said on the point of dying to his sister: 'That opening is so narrow!'

She called out to her mother – my real grandmother, whom she'd lost as a little girl – impatiently: 'Come and get me!' as if her mother were taking her time, keeping her waiting for too long. It must be that the difficulty of dying is the difficulty of living: 'la difficulté d'être'.

Already with her, at the time, I wanted to feel her experience as my own, I tried to pick up every word. Suddenly, she talked to me alone, assigned me a task. This came across as unexpected in our family, where I wasn't seen as having much of an ability to make myself useful. The task was grave, even though it was expressed naturally, in her usual manner. 'As soon as I'm dead,' she said, 'you'll loudly read the *Te Deum*.' She wanted a solemn giving of thanks! I read it, once she had breathed her last, standing at the foot of the bed, amid all the other kneeling women of the house.

Innocenzo did not have that happy lightness of hers; and yet I know that he was infinitely thankful for his life and surely for his death too. But in his long, slow, arduous end he was already situated 'further out there', in the rarified, almost unbreathable air of great silences, the one I call of 'farthest seas'.

107

The term 'requiem', a fruitful theme in music, has been familiar to me since childhood. Back then they'd play the 'rechiemeterna' (to write it Meneghello's way). It was often proposed as a short prayer for the dead, both relatives and strangers.

Then, over the years it was Brahms's austere, solemn *German Requiem*, which Innocenzo liked so much (and which I once listened to with Montale in that little room in his first apartment on Via Bigli). And even earlier, Mozart's tremendous *Funeral Mass*, Verdi's powerful *Mass*.

Hearing the *Dies irae*, in particular, marked the start of my school days. Walking from our house in the rural Orti area towards school in the old part of town, I'd pass the new church and enter for a few minutes. If there was a funeral mass, the orphan girls, standing in the pews, with their little dark capes, would be singing. I hear again, distinctly, their sibilant *s*'s: 'teste David cum Sybilla'. It was mysterious: it didn't even sound like Latin to me (used as I was to Caesar and Cicero).

I had my first *Requiem* after Innocenzo in March (with the bass Raimondi). I thought then that I wanted to call this 'lamentation' *Requiem*; but I know the meaning would be misinterpreted.

Only Antonio understood. 'I know,' he said that day in Campale, while we were looking for strawberries along the riverbank. 'You want it to mean *Hymn*.'

108

For All Saints I returned with Luciana to Demonte, which now for me means to Innocenzo. We also walked along a short mule track covered in dry leaves all the way up to the hollow above the cemetery, invisible from below. Red trees – wild cherries – were blooming here and there at the edges of the meadow like on the banks of a lake.

It always gives me a kind of happiness to think he is up there. The year before, we'd looked at the cemetery together, from the Madonna del Colletto (we'd gone for the commemoration of the Resistance in the Stura and Gesso Valleys). Our architect-surveyor was there and I'd asked him – 'without the slightest suspicion' – to prepare our grave. I had shown the cemetery to the girlfriends I'd met up there; they recalled *The Penumbra* and my love for that place from my childhood. Seen from that perspective, it looked like a second village, a double, as indeed it is, hidden and protected by the hill of the ruined castle.

I returned to Demonte with Piero, too, and I admired how sunny our corner was. 'Eventually they'll build a condominium next to it,' Piero said. The surveyor was with us and he couldn't help but smile; but he said that there was no danger of that happening, because next to the grave they planned to make an opening for the cemetery's future expansion.

Emiliano didn't get permission to come with us, but he had woken up very early to make a flower out of metal wire for us to bring to Grandpa. We slid it into a black poplar vase. On the way back to Demonte with Piero, I showed him the house where I was born – we had it there in front of us – and then in Cuneo, on Viale degli Angeli, the house where he was born.

109

I had told the surveyor that I wanted my name on the grave too; he had replied that it couldn't be done. I didn't ask whether this was for bureaucratic reasons, rules that are in general absurd but final; then I imagined it was a question of propriety. A few months later, I found my name, to the right of his. Not my official name, which my father had chosen for me, but the one I've always been called by. It was a great joy. I didn't ask, but I'm grateful to that young man for having understood.

In an old poem, from our first years together in Cuneo, I'd written: 'I think we will sleep side by side / under the same stone'. It was one of the many premonitions which, in that still-youthful period, thronged my imagination. It was a vision of closeness and at the same time of extreme separateness:

> …and if even there I'm troubled
> by dreams, I will stretch out a hand
> to touch your hand: it will be cold
> as stone, and cold your recumbent
> face, and you will not answer me.

But we won't be next to one another. Under the stone are two burial compartments which are not side by side, but laid one on top of the other. They asked me: 'Should we put him above or below?' I said: 'In sleeping cars, I would go above and he below. Do it that way.'

AFTERWORD
1994

I had come to a dividing line in my life. I didn't know it, but I feared it; there's proof of this in the notes I wrote in Camogli and which I called 'mortal' (*Minima mortalia*).

After, I was swept up as though in a wave. I felt an urgency that didn't have to do – I thought – with writing. But that urgency guided and dictated my writing like a silent voice. I felt as if I were the one who had to pass out of existence, as if the other passing had not already taken place.

A certain urgency, for that matter, is always behind the start of each new book of mine. I need it to get past my defensive indolence, my strong reluctance to face the labour of writing. Here the urgency allowed for – or rather, provoked – a pressing rhythm.

The sense of loss could not be escaped. Writing took the form of an accumulation, but as though it were only temporary – that is, once again, urgent.

What did I grab onto here and there, so as not to be overcome? To crude, merciless, often comical things. This accumulation and this urgency were alternated with pauses, areas of suspension.

Some readers – this was passed on to me, and one even wrote to me – were appalled by certain passages and by my choice of language. After slight astonishment, I dismissed the fact as irrelevant. Actually, it confirmed the necessity of those passages and that language. I won't cite reasons of style in favour of those extreme *points*, which were seen, I suppose, as 'too realistic'. It's not that they should be tolerated because they're counterbalanced by other passages that I wrote: these *points* are what carry, what justify the whole.

It is never the events, nor is it the language, that give meaning to a book. What I've called pauses, and which are returns, reflections – questions and answers to myself – contain, I believe, the reasons for this story. They are the voice that I gave to the infinite silence that had swallowed me whole.

I wrote the first, shorter part after finishing the second. It was 'the backstory', the beginning of our life together and, looking back 'after', it appeared to me full of premonitions.

Here and there lines of poetry emerge (almost all of them familiar to my readers). Those poems assumed an unforeseeable substance. The first part of the book ends with the opening stanza of one of the poems, perhaps the most 'definitive' from my brief career as a poet in verse. I thought that it had to serve as the start of the second part too. It contains the disorientation of our animality and also the humiliation of our logic. Before what? Before what we call 'the eternal'.

> We did not know
> That the eternal is a tempest.

L. R.
March 1994

NOTES

p. 9   *It was Silvia*: Silvia Romano (1910–72) was one of Lalla Romano's two younger sisters, along with Luciana (1922–2009).

p. 10   *the Colonel of the Carabinieri*: The Carabinieri, officially part of Italy's armed forces, constitute one of the principal branches of Italian law enforcement and operate as a national police force.

p. 14   *Minnehaha... Salgari's books*: Emilio Salgari (1862–1911) was an Italian writer of exceptionally popular adventure novels. Minnehaha was the protagonist of the second novel in his series *Avventure nel Far-West* (Adventures in the Far West).

p. 15   *that other fateful one with Giovanni*: In her 1979 book *Una giovinezza inventata* (An Invented Youth), which explores her years as a student at the University of Turin, Romano starts to see a philosophy student named Giovanni Oneglia following an initial discussion about Immanuel Kant. The character was based on Giovanni Ermiglia (1905–2004), a future activist and philosophy teacher.

p. 16   *Lionello Venturi*: Lalla Romano developed a close relationship with the influential art historian and critic Lionello Venturi (1885–1961) after attending his lectures in Turin, as recounted in *Una giovinezza inventata*.

p. 18   *the great Mezzalama*: Ottorino Mezzalama (1888–1931) was an Italian mountain climber who pioneered ski mountaineering in Italy.

p. 24   *moeurs de province*: French for 'provincial mores' or 'provincial manners'. Although Romano is likely not making a direct reference to the novel, *Moeurs de province* was the original subtitle of Gustave Flaubert's *Madame Bovary*.

p. 29   *Superga... my outing with Andrée*: A reference to Romano's French roommate in *Una giovinezza inventata* and to their day trip to Superga, which overlooks Turin.

p. 31   *He's like Cavour*: Camillo Benso, Count of Cavour (1810–61), simply known as Cavour, was a central figure in the unification of Italy.

p. 32   *They will no longer be husbands and wives*: While this quotation is identifiable as Matthew 22:30, the wording Romano uses varies from standard Italian translations of the Gospels. Here as elsewhere in the translation, quoted passages closely reflect the Italian quotations recalled by Romano, rather than more common English versions of the cited texts or films, due to the importance Romano grants to personal memory and to specific word choices.

p. 32   *Enzo Paci*: Enzo Paci (1911–76), an Italian philosopher, was particularly influential for his writings on phenomenology. He and Romano met in their youth while they were both living in Cuneo.

p. 43   *that boy of Bresson's… 'the devil, probably'*: *The Devil, Probably* is a 1977 film by French director Robert Bresson, which ends with the young protagonist dying by assisted suicide. Romano's quotation strays slightly from the French dialogue in the film; a more literal translation of the character's final words would be: 'Do you want me to tell you?'

p. 45   *we never made it to Malga Cengledin*: A *malga* is a high Alpine farmstead or group of pastures, often used as a destination by hikers; the one in question is located outside the town of Trione di Trento, in the Trentino region.

p. 46   *with baby Emiliano*: A reference to Lalla Romano's only grandchild, Emiliano Monti (b. 1970), the son of Piero Monti and his first wife, Marlène. He is a focus of Romano's 1973 novel *L'ospite* (The Guest) and her 1981 novel *Inseparabile* (Inseparable), which recounts Piero and Marlène's divorce during his childhood.

p. 50   *(from* Maria*)*: *Maria*, published in 1953, was Lalla Romano's first novel. It centres on Maria Bottero, a woman from the poor Alpine village of Villar who worked as a maid and nanny for the Romano-Monti family, and who is referred to throughout Romano's work simply by her first name.

p. 53   *By a rough hand… windswept roads*: This is the first stanza of an untitled poem taken from Romano's 1974 poetry collection *Giovane è il tempo* (Time Is Young), a book largely consisting of revised versions of previously published poems from Romano's 1941 collection *Fiore* (Flower) and her 1955 collection *L'autunno* (Autumn), as well as of previously unpublished poems, many of which dated back to the early years of her relationship with Innocenzo Monti.

p. 55 *at the Faithful Companions*: While studying at the University of Turin in the 1920s, Romano lived in the dormitories of the Faithful Companions of Jesus, which was run by nuns.

p. 57 A Silence Shared: Romano's 1957 novel *Tetto Murato*, which was published in Brian Robert Moore's English translation as *A Silence Shared*, closely mirrors many of Romano's own experiences during the German occupation of Italy and the Partisan Resistance. Death is a central theme in the novel not only for the war, but also for the mysterious illness of the character Paolo, a Partisan in hiding whom the narrator, Giulia, looks after along with his wife, Ada, in a remote hamlet called Tetto Murato.

p. 58 *Through the trees… walk off*: The first two lines of an untitled poem that was published in Romano's *Giovane è il tempo*, after originally appearing in a different form in *Fiore* with the title 'Gli uccelli' (The Birds).

p. 61 *'What's worse than robbing a bank?'… Brecht*: A loose reference to Bertolt Brecht's *The Threepenny Opera* (Act 3, Scene 3); the line can be translated in its entirety as 'What is robbing a bank compared to founding a bank?'

p. 61 *I'd remember Eugenia… at Tetto Murato*: Eugenia and Adolfo Ruata were the inspiration for the characters Ada and Paolo in Lalla Romano's *A Silence Shared* (*Tetto Murato*).

p. 63 *(and then Mario)… 'Baj sequuntur?'*: Mario Baj (1907–79), Lalla Romano's brother-in-law, was the husband of her sister Silvia. In this memory, Romano is asking in Latin whether Silvia and Mario Baj are still following them.

p. 65 The Guest: *L'ospite* is a 1973 novel by Romano exploring her relationship with her infant grandson, Emiliano.

p. 65 *the manuscript of* The Penumbra: *La penombra che abbiamo attraversato* is a 1964 novel focusing on Romano's childhood memories of Demonte – a village in the province of Cuneo which is given the fictional name Ponte Stura, after its location in the Stura Valley – where her family lived for the first decade of her life, before moving to the town of Cuneo. It was published in Siân Williams's English translation as *The Penumbra*; although the book's Italian title would translate in full to 'The Penumbra We Have Crossed', in this passage Romano refers to the novel only by the first two words of its title, *La penombra*.

p. 65 *his rediscovered photos from Demonte*: Lalla Romano published a series of notably avant-garde books in which her writing accompanies photographs taken by her father, Roberto Romano, during her childhood in Demonte. The first of these books, *Lettura di un'immagine* (The Reading of an Image) was published in 1975, and, following the discovery of the original photographic plates, a second version titled *Romanzo di figure* (Novel of Figures) was published in 1986. Of these books, Romano stated that 'the images are the text, and the writing an illustration'.

p. 66 *The poem 'We went lightly'*: This poem, which opens with the line 'Noi andavamo leggeri' ('We went lightly'), first appeared in Romano's collection *Fiore* with the title 'Il giardino' (The Garden), and was republished, untitled, in *Giovane è il tempo*. In its final form, it ends with the stanza: 'Your hand waved at me through the plants / but it was a crescent moon / in the distance setting'.

p. 68 *Of nights, love… in us to last.* This canzonet was a previously unpublished poem by Romano.

p. 68 *Simone de Beauvoir… 'le désir mort'*: French for 'dead desire'. Although Romano does not specify the exact source of this quotation, it is in keeping with Simone de Beauvoir, who in *The Second Sex* wrote of the inevitable disappearance of sexual desire over time, particularly for married couples, specifying that '*l'attrait érotique… meurt presque aussi sûrement dans l'estime et l'amitié*' ('erotic attraction… dies almost as surely in esteem and friendship').

p. 69 *In Duras (*L'Amant*): 'la jouissance qui fait crier'*: This is rendered in Barbara Bray's English translation of Marguerite Duras's *The Lover* as 'the pleasure that makes you cry out'. However, the French word *jouissance* is more explicitly associated with orgasms than the more generic English word 'pleasure'.

p. 69 *'Mature men… an aphorism of Pavese's*: The writer, translator and editor Cesare Pavese (1908–50) originally met Romano while they were both students at the University of Turin. He, along with his colleague at the Einaudi publishing house Natalia Ginzburg, would later suggest Romano's first prose book, *Le metamorfosi* (The Metamorphoses), for publication. Romano specifies in her collection of essays and articles *Un sogno del Nord* (A Dream of the North) that the cited aphorism was one Pavese used in conversation rather than in his writing.

p. 69 *no one can rob us… vein in stone*: The entirety of an untitled poem that was published in *Giovane è il tempo*, after originally appearing in a different form in *Fiore* with the title 'La gioia' (Joy). Unlike in

Giovane è il tempo, here Romano does not capitalize the first letter of the first word of the poem.

p. 70 *with Itala and Antonio*: The work of Italian writer and scholar Itala Vivan (b. 1936) largely focuses on African history and culture. The photographer Antonio Ria (b. 1945) first collaborated with Lalla Romano on her 1986 photo text *La treccia di Tatiana* (Tatiana's Braid); following his and Itala Vivan's divorce and the death of Innocenzo Monti, he became Romano's companion until her death in 2001.

p. 70 *Eva and Luigi at the Soldato*: Luigi Rognoni (1913–86) was an Italian musicologist and musical director; his wife, Eva Nibbi Randi, died of suicide in a hotel room in 1970. Il Soldato d'Italia was a trattoria on Via Fiori Chiari, near Lalla Romano and Innocenzo Monti's home in the Brera neighbourhood of Milan.

p. 71 *the naughty girl... her letters in tears*: Fragments of an unpublished poem by Romano.

p. 72 *a talk given by Maria Corti*: Maria Corti (1915–2002) was an influential Italian literary scholar, novelist and semiologist.

p. 73 *Piero as a little boy... in Turin*: Pietro Monti (1933–2018), called Piero, was Lalla Romano and Innocenzo Monti's only child. He appears in many of Romano's books, but is the focus of her 1969 novel *Le parole tra noi leggere* (Light Words Between Us), in which a similar scene is recounted from when the family was living in Turin from 1935 to 1943.

p. 74 *He brought little Andreina*: A reference to Romano's niece Andreina Baj (b. 1947) – the daughter of her sister Silvia and Mario Baj – to whom Innocenzo was particularly attached.

p. 78 *the kind they call 'babbi'... Vittorini*: The writer and translator Elio Vittorini (1908–66) worked for the Einaudi publishing house as the editor of the 'Gettoni' series, which included Romano's first two prose books, *Le metamorfosi* and *Maria*. The word *babbi* is a Sicilian rather than standard Italian term.

p. 79 *my Man Who Talked Alone*: *L'uomo che parlava solo* (The Man Who Talked Alone), published in 1961, is narrated by a middle-aged man after he has fallen out of love with his wife, Nora, and failed to maintain a relationship with a younger woman named Alda. It is Romano's only novel narrated from the perspective of a fictional character whose biography does not directly overlap with her own.

p. 80   *in our home on Via Signorelli*: The Romano-Monti family moved to Via Signorelli 17, their first home in Milan, in 1947, before moving to a more centrally located apartment at Via Brera 17 in the 1950s.

p. 82   *Bacchelli was very amusing*: Riccardo Bacchelli (1891–1985) was an Italian writer whose historical novels reached a large readership and critical acclaim, although their popularity dwindled significantly by the end of his life.

p. 83   *I had recounted dreams… the epic scope of Fenoglio*: References to Romano's first three book-length works of prose: the 1951 collection *Le metamorfosi*, the 1953 novel *Maria* and the 1957 novel *A Silence Shared* (*Tetto Murato*), whose understated treatment of the Resistance she places in contrast with the novels of Beppe Fenoglio (1922–63) – much of Romano's direct involvement in the movement, for instance, is not reflected in the novel. Translating Gustave Flaubert's *Three Tales* during the war was a revelatory experience for Romano, especially the story 'A Simple Heart', which, like *Maria*, focuses on a maid; Flaubert wrote in an 1854 letter: 'One can put an immense love in the story of a blade of grass.'

p. 92   *Casorati said about him*: Felice Casorati (1883–1963) was one of the most important Italian painters of the first half of the twentieth century. Romano studied under him as a painter in Turin, an experience she wrote about in *Una giovinezza inventata*.

p. 95   *the ancient baying… soul's naked fields*: The last three lines of an untitled poem published in Romano's *Giovane è il tempo*.

p. 99   The Metamorphoses… *'The Other'*: *Le metamorfosi*, a collection of stories – all of which are dreams – narrated by multiple characters, was published as Romano's first book-length work of prose in 1951. The original title of this story is 'L'altro'.

p. 101 *on peut péter*: French for 'one can fart'.

p. 103 *Count Lanza… Mrs Abbozzo*: Lodovico Lanza was an Italian architect best known for his activity as a rare-book collector. Annamaria Abbozzo presumably befriended Innocenzo Monti and Lalla Romano through her husband, the banker Giorgio Abbozzo, a colleague of Innocenzo's at Banca Commerciale Italiana.

p. 103 *Mattioli (Raffaele)*: Raffaele Mattioli (1895–1973) was an Italian banker, economist and art patron who, as CEO of Banca Commerciale Italiana for three decades, became perhaps the most influential figure in the history of the bank and spearheaded its support for the arts. He was the father of the book publisher Maurizio Mattioli

(1925–2020), referenced earlier in the chapter and elsewhere in the book.

p. 111 *the Einaudi edition of Philippson's book*: Paula Philippson (1874–1949) was a German classicist whose book *Origini e forme del mito greco* (Origins and Forms of Greek Myth) was published by Einaudi in 1949.

p. 115 *une odeur fade*: French for 'a bland odour'.

p. 117 *a Grand Hotel*: The Grand Hotel Royal in Courmayeur, a more popular and accessible vacation town than Lalla Romano and Innocenzo Monti's previous destinations in the Aosta Valley region: Cheneil, where for years the couple spent part of their summers, and Saint-Nicolas, where they would often take weekend trips.

p. 119 *Mimmina Foà*: Mimmina Foà was the wife of Italian book publisher Luciano Foà, who worked for the Einaudi publishing house before co-founding, in 1962, Adelphi Edizioni, which would become one of Italy's most prestigious literary presses; although she engaged with Luciano's work, she did not play an official role at either house.

p. 129 *you go far off... desperately cry your name*: This is the entirety of an untitled poem taken from *Giovane è il tempo*, though Romano has removed capitalizations and stanza breaks: in *Giovane è il tempo*, the first letters in the first, fourth and sixth lines are capitalized and they begin new stanzas. The poem originally appeared in a different form in Romano's collection *L'autunno* with the title 'Il nome' (The Name).

p. 143 *Storoni's words about Marcus Aurelius*: Lidia Storoni Mazzolani (1911–2006) was an Italian writer, translator and classicist. This is most likely a reference to Storoni Mazzolani's preface to her Italian translation of Walter Pater's *Marius the Epicurean*, which was commissioned by Cesare Pavese for the Einaudi publishing house in the 1930s and republished in 1970: 'Marcus Aurelius reveals (to Marius) the intense interior life, the detachment from worldly things, the self-control and the total renunciation that belong to the stoic; but also the profound, irremediable melancholy of he who has neither hope nor affection: only serene, resigned clear-sightedness and gentle indulgence. And his passive acceptance of harm... and his desperate powerlessness in the face of his son's death, reveal the inability of stoicism to explain essential problems, to alleviate unconquerable harm, to console men in the face of death.'

p. 147 *as Savinio said*: Alberto Savinio (1891–1952), born Andrea Francesco Alberto de Chirico, was a Greek-born Italian painter and writer, and the brother of painter Giorgio de Chirico, with whose work his paintings share many surreal and dreamlike qualities.

p. 148 *We did not know… arctic wind*: The first stanza of an untitled poem published in Romano's *Giovane è il tempo*.

p. 149 *Liliana, the only person who knew him well*: Innocenzo Monti's secretary at Banca Commerciale Italiana until his retirement from the role of president in 1981.

p. 152 *Marlène had come with the children*: Marlène was Piero Monti's first wife and the mother of Romano's grandson, Emiliano Monti. The children in question are Emiliano, and Marlène's second child, Olmo, whom she had following her and Piero's divorce, as recounted in *Inseparabile*.

p. 152 *Gramigna recreated in his* Impious Aeneas: *Empio Enea* is a formally experimental novel by Italian writer Giuliano Gramigna (1920–2006) published in 1972. Never translated into English, it has largely been forgotten in Italy, too.

p. 153 *Ettore came*: A reference to classicist Ettore Cingano, the son of the CEO of Banca Commerciale Italiana Francesco Cingano, with whose family Innocenzo Monti developed a close relationship over the years.

p. 162 *Thus, through Tullia*: The partner and, later, second wife of Lalla Romano's son, Piero Monti (the couple married in 1994).

p. 164 *Carlo Bombieri… Lella Solmi… Bruna Cingano*: Present at the funeral are important colleagues of Innocenzo's from Banca Commerciale Italiana as well as their family members whom he had befriended: Carlo Bombieri was the bank's CEO from 1965 to 1973; the literary scholar Raffaella (Lella) Solmi (b. 1956) collaborated on scholarly work with her father, the celebrated poet and essayist Sergio Solmi (1899–1981), who was a lawyer and legal adviser for the bank; Bruna Cingano (née Carisi) was the wife of Francesco Cingano, the bank's CEO at the time of Innocenzo's death in 1984.

p. 164 *the Levi-Montalcini sisters*: Paola Levi-Montalcini (1909–2000) was an Italian painter whom Lalla Romano befriended while they were both studying at Felice Casorati's painting school in Turin. Her twin sister, Rita Levi-Montalicini (1909–2012), was an Italian neurobiologist who won the 1986 Nobel Prize in Physiology or Medicine.

p. 164 *She was Leda, Ugo's wife*: Ugo Chiodoni often appears as Piero Monti's close friend from school in *Le parole tra noi leggere*, in which he is generally referred to by his last name only.

p. 166 *Giulio Einaudi: he hadn't listened to Innocenzo in life*: Giulio Einaudi (1912–99) was likely the most important Italian book publisher of the twentieth century. In 1933 he founded Einaudi Editore, which would go on to publish nearly all of Lalla Romano's books. Innocenzo Monti often attempted to give financial advice to Giulio Einaudi during periods of financial difficulty for the publishing house.

p. 168 *the character from* Light Words Between Us: *Le parole tra noi leggere*, Romano's 1969 novel focusing on her relationship with her son, Piero, became a bestseller after it won the Strega Prize, Italy's most prestigious literary award. The success of the book, which made ample use of Piero's letters and other personal material, caused their relationship to deteriorate.

p. 172 *that little girl of Ortese's after she put on glasses*: A reference to the story 'Un paio di occhiali' – translated by Ann Goldstein and Jenny McPhee as 'A Pair of Eyeglasses' – by Italian writer Anna Maria Ortese (1914–98) from her collection *Il mare non bagna Napoli*, which was published in English as *Evening Descends Upon the Hills* and *Neapolitan Chronicles*.

p. 172 *I recalled* Teorema: The Italian writer and filmmaker Pier Paolo Pasolini (1922–75) directed a 1968 film tilted *Teorema* and wrote a 1968 novel of the same title, which was published in Stuart Hood's English translation as *Theorem*. The unnamed, 'perfect being' in question is the character called '*l'ospite*' ('the guest'), played in the film version by Terence Stamp.

p. 172 *that has no end… night pierces*: A fragment of an unpublished poem by Romano.

p. 173 *Saglio, in that discreetly fraternal way*: Likely a reference to Gianfranco Saglio, a colleague of Innocenzo's at Banca Commerciale Italiana and the secretary of the bank's board of directors at the time of his death.

p. 174 *I loved without malice, but without measure*: This line likely originates from a loose Italian translation of 'Of one that loved not wisely, but too well' (*Othello*, Act 5, Scene 2). In Romano's early notes for the book, the words '*ho amato*' ('I loved') are left outside of the quotation marks, meaning this sentence in the Italian translation of *Othello* might not have been in the first person and therefore would have been more consistent with Shakespeare's original.

p. 177 *Meneghello's way*: Luigi Meneghello (1922–2007) was an Italian writer and scholar who frequently used non-standard and dialectal spellings in his writing, beginning with his first book, *Libera nos a Malo*, which was published in Frederika Randall's English translation as *Deliver Us*.

p. 177 *Montale… on Via Bigli*: The Italian poet Eugenio Montale (1896–1981), who won the Nobel Prize for Literature in 1975, met Lalla Romano in 1940, before the publication of her first poetry collection. He later became an outspoken admirer of her prose, especially for its poetic qualities, writing favourable reviews of several of her novels. He lived in two apartments on Via Bigli in Milan, first at number 11 and then at number 15.

p. 180 *I think we will sleep… you will not answer me*: These lines are taken from an untitled poem that was published in Romano's *Giovane è il tempo*, after originally appearing in a different form in *Fiore* with the title 'I campi eterni' (The Eternal Fields).